KiLL aLL HAPPIES

KiLL aLL

HAPPIES

RACHEL COHN

HYPERION
LOS ANGELES   NEW YORK

Copyright © 2017 by Rachel Cohn

First Edition, May 2017
10 9 8 7 6 5 4 3 2 1
FAC-020093-17076

Printed in the United States of America

This book is set in Palatino/Monotype
Designed by Marci Senders

Library of Congress Cataloging-in-Publication Data
Names: Cohn, Rachel, author.
Title: Kill all Happies / Rachel Cohn.
Description: First edition. | Los Angeles ; New York : Hyperion, 2017. |
    Summary: "In this romantic, contemporary suburban odyssey, Victoria
    Navarro has one night to throw the ultimate graduation party, say
    good-bye to lifelong friends, and make sure her longtime crush never
    forgets her."—Provided by publisher.
Identifiers: LCCN 2016001044| ISBN 9781423157229 (hardcover) |
    ISBN 1423157222 (hardcover)
Subjects: | CYAC: Graduation (School)—Fiction. | Parties—Fiction.
    | Dating (Social customs)—Fiction. | High schools—Fiction. |
    Schools—Fiction.
Classification: LCC PZ7.C6665 Ki 2017 | DDC [Fic]—dc23
LC record available at https://lccn.loc.gov/2016001044

Reinforced binding
Visit www.hyperionteens.com

SUSTAINABLE Certified Sourcing
FORESTRY
INITIATIVE   www.sfiprogram.org
              SFI-00993

THIS LABEL APPLIES TO TEXT STOCK

PART ONE

1   WISDOM FROM AN ELDER
A Few Hours Before

Text from Lindsay:

> Hey, dumbslut. Don't throw a party just
> to impress a guy.

This is the story of how I never listen to my big sister.

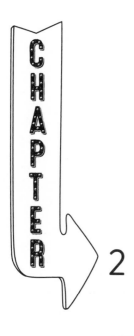

WARPATH OF SUCK

1 a.m.

The face of evil looked so pretty in the moonlight. You'd want to kiss her unless you knew better. Then you'd want to suffocate her.

With a fitness-freak figure, corn-silk blond hair tightened into a bun, and wispy tendrils framing her former beauty-pageant–winning face, people sometimes wondered why the attractive Annette Thrope, Rancho Soldado High School's resident economics teacher, had acquired the nickname "Miss Ann Thrope." They would stop wondering if, for instance, they saw her as I did that night, backlit by a full moon, packing heat and ready to rumble. The pretty lady with the blackest of hearts had arrived at the theme park party ready to do what she did best: ruin everyone's good time.

I found Thrope standing outside the open driver's side door of the Chug Bug, a former VW bus that Jake had spent the past year of his life painstakingly repurposing into a beer truck. The Chug Bug had fueled the opening hours of my senior class party at Happies restaurant, but was now parked at the empty edge of the old Happies theme park's Ravishing Ravine, its headlights offering a faint glimpse into the abyss down below. I didn't know how the Chug Bug had gotten there, but I assumed Jake had moved it to this secluded spot deep in the park as a precaution after the Happies fanatics had stormed the party and dismantled the gates. Anyone besides Thrope would admire the Chug Bug (pimped-out beer cruiser— what wasn't to love?), but if the police arrived next, their vehicle appreciation might quickly wane once they realized that the Chug Bug had been serving the Rancho Soldado High School senior class of underage drinkers all night long.

More fearsome than the potential intrusion of official law enforcement, though, was actual vigilante law enforcement: Thrope. Her eyes were ablaze and she had a rifle slung over her back like she was a late-middle-aged Annie Oakley. The founder of Rancho Soldado's Ladies Rifle Club never traveled unprepared. Nice way to break up a party: pack a weapon and hold the beer truck hostage. Always gunning for popularity, our Miss Ann Thrope.

"Victoria," she hissed. "Are you responsible for this mess?"

My party was so *not* a mess, unless by "mess," Thrope meant a couple hundred newly graduated, highly inebriated classmates reveling in Happies' previously abandoned theme park along with hordes of hardcore Happies fanatics. The crowds roamed the grounds now dotted with litter, puke, and empty bottles, but the real "mess" this night was my gnawing fear that some drunk dumbfuck would light a campfire on this parched, drought-stricken desert land on the California-Nevada border and close out Happies one last time with a literal blaze of glory.

Dear Rancho Soldado High School Class of Two Thousand and Awesome:

You're welcome. Because yes, I personally made this party happen. May tonight's infinite supply of rocky road ice cream nourish your hearts, tingle your cavities, and give you forever-fond memories of Happies after it's demolished to make way for whatever big-box store brings big-time suck to our town in its place. Love and easy does it on the orange marmalade Jell-O shots (thanks, Emerson Luong!),

Your pal and classmate, Vic Navarro

I couldn't let this party take a death dive into Grinchtown just because the ultimate party pooper had arrived. I told Thrope, "If by 'mess' you mean 'amazingness,' then yes, I'm responsible."

Before she could fire another round of accusations at me, Zeke, my night's unexpected companion, dared to ask her, "Um, that's a pellet rifle you have there, right, Ms. Thrope?"

"You'd better hope it is, young man," said Thrope, in a threatening teacher tone that implied, *You may not have been my student yet. But you will be.* Since school let out all of yesterday, Zeke had advanced to high school junior. Thrope walked closer to him, sniffing for alcohol. He exhaled loudly and she quickly retreated back to the Chug Bug. (Boy breath. Not beer breath. I'm guessing.) Then her gaze narrowed onto my face again. "If this is your party, Victoria, I hope you're ready to see it end. Badly."

How badly could it end? Happies was already over. Throughout the park, partygoers were celebrating the Last Call at Happies, before our desert town's most beloved institution was razed to make way for a Monster Mall. I'd worked so hard to ensure Thrope didn't find out about the hastily organized party, but now that she was here, I thought, *So what?* I'd own up to my responsibility, and then some. I told Thrope, "No way am I going to let you ruin my party."

If this party was a mess, it was *my* mess, and I had it under control.

Mostly under control.

Partly under control.

Not really at all under control.

But what could Thrope do to me now? Give me detention? I'd already graduated. It's not like I was counting on her for a college recommendation letter. I'd already been rejected from the one university I'd applied to.

"A beer truck serving minors?" asked Thrope. "Your idea?"

"Pretty much!" I admitted. The Chug Bug had been one of my better economic brainstorms, if I did say so myself. Because of all the money and exposure he'd be getting from it tonight, I felt very confident that the Chug Bug's owner, Jake Zavala-Kim, would be giving me a very generous thank-you. A cash percentage would be nice, but the orgasms would be even better. Once upon a very delicious memory, Jake and I made out while we were locked in the walk-in ice cream freezer back when we both worked as waitstaff at Happies. That random encounter never progressed beyond lip-locking and ass-groping before some jerk had to unlock the door from the outside, but now that I was leaving town for good, I planned to get the deed done and make sure Jake remembered me when I was gone. Really, really remembered me.

"Well, then," Thrope said. "I guess now's the time for you to see how I deal with underage drinkers."

Before I could respond, Zeke said, "Sing-alongs?" It was definitely not the time for joking, but it was impossible not to be inspired by the locals' favorite song being sung by an assembly of drunken celebrants in the park's nearby Pinata Village. Zeke sung along with them:

> *On the LA to Vegas*
> *hop hop hop*
> *Tummies ready for yummies*
> *At everyone's favorite dessert in the desert*
> *stop stop stop!*
> *Happies Happies Happies*
> *Super burgers then ice cream with a toy*
> *Where your happiness is our*
> *joy joy joy*
> *So come to Happies . . . hop hop hop!*

Bold move for a junior, Zeke! Miss Ann Thrope hated nothing more than Happies. Thrope despised a lot about her students—when they were tardy, when they wandered school during class periods without hall passes, when their superior opinions didn't gel with her misinformed ones. Actually, like many high school teachers, what Thrope loathed most was students, *period*. But what really drove

Thrope crazy was when students defiled her classroom with Happies restaurant evidence: Happies sandwich wrappers, Happies drink containers, Happies french fries spelling out FUCK YOU on a desk with a ketchup-drawn heart around the message. Thrope was a notorious health nut, but even that didn't explain the level of hatred she had for all things Happies. It made no sense. She'd once been a Miss Happie!

Encouraged by Zeke, I joined in on the song's last line. *So come to Happies . . . hop hop hop!* On cue, Zeke and I hop-hop-hopped to the last line of the song. Take that, Thrope!

My persistent worry about someone setting a campfire in the park was misplaced. The fury rising on Thrope's face could easily have sparked one instead. But rather than verbally respond, Thrope let out a little chortle, and then she leaned down and into the open door at the Chug Bug's driver's side.

"NOOOO!" Zeke and I both yelled, realizing what she was about to do.

Too late.

Thrope released the Chug Bug's parking brake.

The beer truck lurched forward suddenly, but slowly, creaking as it inched along the road. Zeke and I lunged toward the front of the truck to try to stop its movement, but Cardio-Queen Thrope sprinted to the back of the truck faster and gave it a forceful nudge.

Creak. Rock. Roooooll.

As carelessly as a tiny marble going over a toy mountain, the Chug Bug dropped over the side of the road. But louder. Much, much louder. The truck tumbled down the hill—RUMBLE! BOOM! THUNK!—before landing vertically at the bottom of the ravine. CRASH! The truck was smashed, totaled, dunzo. Yet, somehow, its faceup lights still worked, illuminating the sky like a fucked-up Bat-Signal.

Thrope said, "*That* is how I deal with underage drinking, kiddos."

Zeke looked at me, and I looked at him. There really was only one response. "Fuuuuuuuck," we both said. The sight was horrific, yet bizarrely compelling.

The commotion had caused a swarm of partygoers to come forth to see what had happened, which was more worrisome. The Chug Bug was possibly about to ignite and explode on this drought-ridden land where there was no clear exit path out of a dangerous fire's way for the gathering crowd.

Thrope was the one at fault here. But everyone knew it was my party, my idea . . . and my mess, indeed. Would I go from party hero to party pariah? Had I taunted Thrope into unleashing this destruction? All that beer gone to waste! I feared everyone would blame me—particularly Jake.

It's true. The beer truck was destroyed and the whole park was in danger of igniting, but my true worry was: Would this incident prevent me from getting some at the end of the night? Yes, I am that shallow.

Unconcerned about the destruction she'd caused, Thrope swaggered off on her warpath without so much as a smug look of self-satisfaction back in my direction. She slung her rifle over her shoulder and walked resolutely to face off against my classmates and the Happies biker gang now descending on the Ravishing Ravine. The founder of the Rancho Soldado Ladies Rifle Club was on the hunt.

"What are you going to do now?" I called to Thrope, but what I was really wondering was where the hell were Slick and Fletch? There was no crisis I couldn't handle so long as they were on deck with me.

Thrope removed her rifle from its sling and cocked it onto her shoulder. She turned back around to tell me, "I'm putting an end to this party once and for all. It's time to kill all Happies."

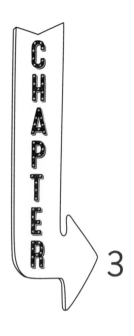

CHAPTER 3

GRADUATION
CEREMONY CRYFEST

3:30 p.m., The Day Before

Since kindergarten, we did things in threes. Victoria Navarro, Genesis Fletcher, and Mercedes Zavala-Kim, aka Vic, Fletch, and Slick. Team Cuddle Huddle.

Yet, there was our Fletch, standing alone at the podium of our high school graduation ceremony, delivering a solo valedictorian speech. Slick and I did not have the academic qualifications to help her. We weren't in the honor society. Not Merit Scholars. Not even in the top 10 percent of our class rank. We were more like top 30 percent (me) and barely squeaking into the top 50 percent (Slick). Fletch would have to emote from up there at the podium without her two BFFs, who could only watch her from the audience, choking back tears of pride.

But Slick and I were more than happy for Fletch to lead us into the future. No one else in Rancho Soldado High School's graduating class even approached Fletch on the scale of godliness. She had come so far to get here. An orphan adopted from an African refugee camp at the age of five by a newly married couple doing humanitarian work, Genesis didn't speak a word of English when she first arrived in America. She was too small, malnourished and had already witnessed the worst the world had to offer before she'd even stepped one tiny foot into a school-room. Now look at her. She was nearly six feet tall—long, lean, and gorgeous. She could have been a fashion model but she'd opted to defer her merit scholarship to Yale so she could follow in her parents' footsteps. She'd spend the next year doing humanitarian work in the country of her birth.

As Fletch pontificated about kindness, strength, dignity, and responsibility, Slick texted me from the T–Z row of chairs, several rows back from my L–N row. Gawd, I've never been so proud.

I typed back. No shit. Her awesomeness defies the law of gravity.

Slick: I swear I can feel the universe tilting as Fletch speaks.

Me: I can't believe her new head.

What couldn't Fletch pull off, including this epic show?

Slick: Seriously. You also had no clue she was going to do it?

Me: Nope. Big violation of the Cuddle Huddle code, but forgivable.

Slick: We probably would have tried to talk her out of it.

Me: True.

Slick: I love our baldy so much.

A tear fell onto my phone, making it difficult for me to type on the wet surface. My determined fingers managed to bang out the message anyway: OUR BALDY IS GOING TO RUN THE WORLD ONE DAY!

Fletch had arrived to the graduation ceremony with a shocking new look. She'd razor-cut her hair in honor of her imminent departure for Africa the day after next. Her new head of hair was barely that, about the length of a pinky fingernail—just the moon part. Her new do was fierce, bold, miraculous—just like her.

I turned around to catch a glimpse of Fletch's parents in the stands. Reverend Doctor Cedric Fletcher was standing in the aisle, recording Fletch's speech on his phone, weeping, while Fletch's mom, Dr. Erika Fletcher, #1-ranked pediatrician in *Las Vegas* magazine, sat on the aisle seat next to him. They were a family of benevolent overachievers. It was always interesting to see Fletch and her parents standing side by side. Fletch had her mom's dark skin tone and her dad's height, none of their facial features, and all of their confident, articulate mannerisms.

Mrs. Dr. Fletcher also wept, probably as much with pride as with grief, for she'd been the one washing, combing, oiling, and braiding Fletch's hair since her Genesis was a little girl.

I sent a text to my dad, sitting in the row ahead of the Fletchers. Record the end of our girl's speech on your phone, ok? (I could record it on my own, of course, but I was too busy texting.) The Reverend is crying so hard his phone is probably shaking and I'm sure he'd appreciate a better recording.

On it, Dad typed back. I found my father's face in the audience, and watched him raise his phone to record. I lifted a thumbs-up in his direction, and that seemed to be Dad's cue to sob. Sitting next to him on either side, my twenty-three-year-old twin siblings, Lindsay and Chester, lifted their middle fingers to me, and I laughed. They'd be in tears by the end of the ceremony, too. If they had any decency. I sighed. They didn't. My people, bless 'em.

Fletch told the audience, "As Winston Churchill once said: 'If you're going through hell, keep going.' I love you all. Congratulations, and happy graduation!"

The graduating class jumped to its feet, applauding wildly at the conclusion of Fletch's speech. That is, I jumped to my feet, as did Slick, and Fletch's ex, Olivier Farkas. So I flailed my arms, inviting our classmates to join us, and they politely accommodated me, rising to their feet to cheer. Not for nothing was my hometown nickname "General Navarro." My academic class standing may have been lukewarm at best, but I knew how to rally troops. Standing O for our girl, who deserved no less.

Next, Principal Carillo returned to the podium. "Thank you for the inspiration, Genesis Fletcher. Just excellent." He beamed at Fletch, who sat down at her seat on the dais of honored guests and nodded at him serenely, as if to say, *Of course it was excellent. I would accept no less from myself.* Principal Carillo returned his gaze to the graduating class. "Now, please join me in welcoming Rancho Soldado's mayor, the Honorable Jerry Finkel."

Our mayor stepped to the podium as several classmates whooped and hollered for him, shouting out "Mayor Jerry!" The seniors doing the whooping were definitely those with the silver flasks hidden beneath their graduation gowns, but the sentiment was sincere, sober or not. Everyone loved Mayor Jerry, except Miss Ann Thrope, who was sitting in the front row so I couldn't see her face, but was probably scowling at Mayor Jerry's warm reception before he'd even said a word. Thrope, who was also the Town Council chairwoman, had spent the past decade battling every initiative Mayor Jerry had tried to pass for the town's benefit. No wonder he was retiring. He had better ways to spend his time than futile efforts to better our town and being bullied by Thrope. He was giving up his mayoral seat to focus on his men's novelty shirt store, Tunics of Virility, to enjoy his impending fatherhood, and to write *Doctor Who* fanfic.

Sartorially, Mayor Jerry had gone all out to honor the occasion of the last Rancho Soldado High School graduating class under his jurisdiction. It was the first time I'd seen him not looking like a hobo. He usually dressed in dirty, baggy, holey pants and a loud Hawaiian shirt picturing palm trees or surfers or half-naked hula girls. But today, he wore a pair of beige chinos that were about an inch too short on his legs but actually fit around his waist— the pants may even have been new!—and a wrinkled pink-and-green-striped oxford shirt. The too-short pants' length gave a good glimpse of his sockless ankles and open-toed man sandals. He might have looked fashionably faux preppy except for his ivory-colored, 1970s-style wide necktie that was loose around his neck and fell closer to his rib line than his stomach. His shoulder-length, mangy salt-and-pepper hair was not brushed—thank God, or I really would have worried about him—but it was pulled back in a ponytail, tied with what appeared to be red Christmas wrapping ribbon.

Mayor Jerry held out his arms to us and smiled. "Ya made it!" he said, and the class cheered.

Text blast from my sister, Lindsay: Ha-ha! Someone just asked Jon Z-K for an autograph!

I turned around again to see Slick's parents, Jon and Selena Zavala-Kim, sitting in the row ahead of my family. Someone's grandma stood in the aisle, fanning herself with her hand, while Jon Z-K signed what appeared to be the graduation ceremony program handout. Slick's head was also turned around to witness this abomination. Ugh, Slick texted me. Her father was a local celebrity, and it was impossible not to recognize him today. His weirdly handsome face (weird because he was a dad) loomed large over the occasion, prominently displayed on a large highway billboard in the distance behind the football field. Wearing a loud vintage bowling shirt, Jon Z-K was the advertising face of Tunics of Virility. Everyone suspected Mayor Jerry spent more on that billboard than he earned at the store in a year. (The mayor was probably the only independently wealthy trust fund baby in mostly working-class Rancho Soldado.)

Mayor Jerry read his speech from his phone, but everyone knew the phone was really there just in case he got a text from Sheriff Cheryl, whose wife, Darlene, was due to go into labor any minute. Mayor Jerry was the sperm donor.

Mayor Jerry said, "Today we're here to celebrate our town's latest graduating class, but also to confer an honorary degree on one of Rancho Soldado's most distinguished and beloved townspeople. Her name has been synonymous with Rancho Soldado since her grandparents' first highway pie stand so many years ago. It was that road stand's famous RASmatazz pies that eventually gave birth to the Happies restaurant and then the sorely missed Happies theme park. A lot of you might not know that this high school where we're celebrating today is actually the second incarnation of Rancho Soldado High School. The original building burned down during a particularly bad brush-fire season sixty years ago, and one of its students opted to go work at the family restaurant rather than wait for the new school to be built. She took her own damn time about it, as she would say, but a few months ago, I'm delighted to tell you that at the young age of seventy-five, Ms. Bev Happie passed her GED test."

More hoots and hollers from the audience. *Go, Bev! Hell yeah, Bev!* (Nothing honored Bev more than cursing.) Mayor Jerry continued, "Today we pay tribute to her and the proud legacy to Rancho Soldado that the Happies institution brought us all. Beverly Olivia Happie, could you please step forward now so I may confer on you your freaking high school degree!"

This time there was no need for me to rally the audience. My classmates and everyone in the stands immediately rose to their feet, clapping and cheering, as Bev Happie walked from the dais to the podium, wearing a cap and gown with Happies insignias stitched around the collar. Mayor Jerry, grinning, moved the tassel on Bev's mortarboard from the right to the left, and then handed her a diploma.

Bev Happie was a member of our graduating class! Obviously, we were the greatest graduating class in the history of Rancho Soldado High School.

It took a few minutes for the claps and cheers to die down and the crowd to return to its seats so Bev could address us.

"Damn it," she said, laughing. "You're giving me a hell of a cry." She cleared her throat and wiped tears from her cheeks. "Thank you, Mayor Jerry, and thank you, Rancho Soldado, for giving Happies its treasured home since my grandparents' time." She looked down at the graduating class. "And you kids," she said fondly. "You little bastards. I love ya!" Many shouts of *We love you too, Bev!* "Generations of Rancho students have worked at Happies, and it's been your youthful energy that kept it alive so long. Never had a family of my own. Didn't need to. You were it. I'm sorry to say that, as you know, Happies closed for good last week. But its memory will live long in our hearts. And you will always be my family—loved, appreciated, occasionally cursed upon when you leave freezer doors open and the ice cream thaws. Thank you, Rancho Soldado. I couldn't be prouder to be one of your high school's graduates."

There was not a dry eye in the house. And it wasn't mere choked-back sobs resounding across the football field. It was more like waves and waves of weeping wails.

That's when I knew. As Mayor Jerry hugged a sobbing Bev Happie, I realized she was at the perfect moment of vulnerability. It had been clear for a while that the Happies restaurant was going under and wouldn't survive the year, and I, its former worst waitress, had relentlessly campaigned for Bev to allow the senior class to retire the restaurant in style, to no avail. Until now. I would beg her one last time to let me throw a senior class party at Happies.

Now was the right moment to pounce. This time she'd say yes.

4

BABY BEV BAWLS
4:30 p.m., The Day Before

"No," said Bev. "Absofuckinglutely not."

After the ceremony, Bev was all but tackled on the football field. Tackled by love. Herds of graduates and their families couldn't leave the festivities until they'd gotten one last hug and signature kiss on the cheek from Bev Happie. I was one of the stragglers at the end of the love parade. I'd waited till I knew Bev would be exhausted but also coasting on goodwill. Then, I'd made my move, going in for a hug, congratulating her, and on the down-low, saying, "Happies should have that one last party, don't you think? Pretty fucking please, Bev?"

I had to speak quietly, because the request was bold. And illegal. For years, Happies had hosted an annual graduation party for the town's high school seniors. But Rancho people party hard, and in some cases too hard. The yearly grad party had been banned five years earlier after it got too rowdy and some "hooligans" (Town Council report's word choice, not mine) took their after-party to the front yard of the home of their most reviled teacher, Annette Thrope. They TP'd her house; a predictably lame stunt which might have been no big deal—except that they also, in their drunken state, tried to dig a well to push her car into and, in the midst of this dumbass mission, they managed to rupture a sewer pipe in Thrope's yard, leading to a very bad, very smelly sludge situation, and very costly damage. A few months later, Thrope pushed the Town Council into pressuring Bev Happie to end the annual party, or risk having Happies' restaurant business operation permits revoked. End of a decades-old tradition. Moral of the story, drunken teens: Don't mess with Thrope. Especially when your former teacher is also the chairwoman of the Town Council. Dumbfucks.

After her adamant "No," Bev placed a kiss on my cheek, and then she whispered into my ear, "Even if you were my favorite terrible waitress, you manipulative dear heart, a last senior class party is just a bad idea, and you and I both know it." She kindly didn't point out that my party idea potentially made me a dumber fuck than the well-diggers from that final Happies graduation party.

An older gentleman who looked around Bev's age approached us, wearing a sash across his chest that was adorned with Happies pins, patches, and rings. He looked like an elderly Boy Scout.

"Incoming Happie," I warned Bev, whose sight wasn't that good. "Happies" was the nickname given by locals to overzealous fans who met each other at small conventions to trade old Happies memorabilia from its heyday, when it was the fun desert destination of choice on the route between Las Vegas and Southern California.

To Bev, the man said, "Congratulations, Miss Happie. I'm an old fan from way back. Almost old enough to remember the pie stand!"

Bev laughed and gave the man a kiss on the cheek. "Thank you from the bottom of my heart," she said. She turned to me and asked, "Do you have a pen, doll?" I searched my purse, expecting, as Bev did, that the man had an old Happies theme park map or Happies restaurant kids' coloring place mat for Bev to autograph. "What would you like me to sign?" Bev asked him.

Instead of a pen, I first pulled a dollar bill from my purse and waved it at Bev, to remind her of how she could get rich. She shook her head at me. Bev never accepted money for her autograph from the Happies fanfolk at conventions—which was a shame, because if she did, the restaurant might not have gone under.

"No autograph," said the man. "Got one from you a few years back at the Happies Midwest Regional. I'm honored you'd offer, but that's not why I came here." He reached into his pants pocket. "I have something for you."

His hand ventured too far into his crotch area. I was about to lunge at the might-be elderly pervert until he pulled out a chain necklace with a locket on it. "I wanted you to have this," he told Bev.

She took the locket, opened it, and fresh tears sprung to her eyes. "Is that a certified Baby Bev?" I asked, admiring the picture inside, a charcoal drawing of an infant with baby black hair and big black eyes rimmed with thick black eyelashes.

"It is," Bev sputtered, genuinely touched. She tried to hand the locket back to the man. "I can't accept it. It's worth too much. Only a dozen were made."

"I know," said the man. "They were given as prizes to the first winners of Happies' Drown a Clown contest on its inaugural day."

"Which was my—"

"—first birthday," they both said.

The man took the locket from Bev's hand and instead of returning it to his pocket, he clasped it around her neck. "Happy graduation," he said. "From the Happies Society,

Local Chapter Minneapolis, Minnesota. We're mighty proud of you." He bowed down to her, and walked away, his mission accomplished.

Now was definitely the moment to ask one more time about the senior class party, but with what minor speck of dignity I had, I didn't. The tender moment should not be interrupted by another shameless request for a party no one besides me cared about anymore. Even I knew that. So I grabbed Bev into another hug, because she looked like she was about to pass out from the afternoon desert heat and the emotion, and a fresh wave of bawling. She needed to lean on someone.

"People can be so gawddamn wonderful sometimes," she said. "Even those crazy Happies fans."

Seeing me in hug posture, my BFFs hovering nearby came forth to fortify the ranks. We'd been named the "Cuddle Huddle" by our kindergarten teacher, who'd randomly assigned me and Slick to be new student Fletch's first school buddies. We'd taken it upon ourselves to immediately wrap the new student into a suffocating threesome hug, which we'd barely broken free from in the intervening years. I opened my arms so Slick and Fletch could join my hug with Bev. We didn't usually let in outsiders to our Cuddle Huddle, but Bev was an exception.

"We're going to miss you so much," Slick said to Bev, who was planning to retire to Florida.

"You *are* Rancho Soldado," Fletch said to Bev. "How can you leave it?"

Bev kicked me in the shin. "*This* bimbo is Rancho Soldado."

I laughed. This bimbo was planning to escape Rancho Soldado even sooner than Bev. In a week, I'd be going to live with my sister, Lindsay, in San Francisco. I was hardly the emblem of Rancho Soldado that Bev was. I couldn't escape it fast enough. Fog and cold breezes and sky-high rent, all wrapped in artisanal toasts and fair trade coffees that cost more than I used to make in Happies waitress tips in an hour? Awesome. Freedom. For-real adulthood. At last.

A finger tapped my shoulder. "Can I get in on the Cuddle Huddle?" a grating female voice asked.

I turned my head to see Evergrace Everdell, still wearing her cap and gown even though most everyone else had ditched theirs by now because of the heat. Technically, Evergrace was also a graduating senior, but she'd been homeschooled since moving to Rancho Soldado a few years earlier. Her parents, New York expats who'd retreated to our California desert town because it was cheap and so they could run an experimental-theater space in their backyard, thought Evergrace was too "sensitive" and "exceptional" for "fascist high school social hierarchies." Despite removing her from our hallowed classrooms of learning, they insisted that Evergrace still be allowed to attend school functions like dances, and to join the Drama Club, the Hobbit Society, the Gay-Straight Alliance, Team LARP, and the Thrope-led Libertarian Young Guns Club. Evergrace's parents threatened to sue the school board if anyone so much as suggested that their daughter should also be a matriculated student in order to participate in school programs.

"No, you can't," I said. The Cuddle Huddle was my sacred tribe, and Evergrace didn't belong in it. She was always whining about inclusiveness, so I figured she needed a reminder of exclusiveness.

"We're *crying* here," said Fletch, refusing admittance to the outsider.

"I'm telling," Evergrace said, like we were five-year-olds instead of newly minted high school graduates. She made a beeline toward Thrope.

I placed my head back inside the Cuddle Huddle.

I really wished I could get Thrope good one last time. It was a family tradition, kind of. My brother, Chester, had been on the crew of the well-digging disaster that had finally killed the Happies graduation party five years earlier. My sister, Lindsay, had helped transport the keg to keep the laborers inspired and refreshed. Of course, they'd participated in a moment of drunken impulse at the end of an epic Happies senior class party. Their instincts may have been right, but if they'd been more sober, maybe they would have settled for a predictable stunt, where the consequences wouldn't have been so damning to future graduating classes of Rancho Soldado High School.

If I couldn't throw a party to dig at Thrope as my final hurrah, I vowed I'd find some other way before I left town. For now, I'd cry with my besties.

5

DON'T CRY FOR THROPE
5 p.m., The Day Before

"Congratulations, Jay," Thrope said to my dad, her face stone cold with insincerity. Thrope did not shake Dad's hand and he did not extend his own to her; indeed, he didn't make eye contact with her, fully aware of her soul-sucking powers. They had a history of mutual contempt. Many people did with Thrope, but in my family's case, the history was more personal.

"Thanks," Dad said, trying to maneuver us toward his car and out of Thrope's life, for good.

Thrope added, "You got all three graduated from high school. Nothing short of a miracle." Certainly Thrope had given the Navarro kids enough unjustified detentions, tardies, and poor grades to make our graduations seem like divine intervention.

Dad said, "Miracles had nothing to do with it."

My brother, Chester, snorted his stoner laugh. *Heh. Heh heh.* Lindsay and I had been decent enough students, but it really *was* a miracle Chester had managed to graduate high school.

Chester took a drag on a cigarette.

"This is a smoke-free school. I trust you'll be quitting that nasty habit, right, Chester?" Thrope asked my brother.

Why did her car have to be parked next to ours? Was this the longest parking lot walk ever?

Chester shrugged. "Maybe," he mumbled. Nobody ever just said "No" to Thrope.

"Not maybe. *Will,*" Thrope said, and this time Lindsay laughed.

Chester had totally set himself up for Thrope's signature retort to any student or Town Council member who dared answer her unreasonable demands with a wishy-washy "Maybe." Thrope then had the audacity to hand her business card to my dad.

"It's a great time to list your house. Call me." You'd think that being the mastermind and lead Realtor of the Happies land sale would have been enough commission for Rancho Soldado's most annoying multitasker, but apparently not.

Dad gave us kids a look like, *Is she kidding?* Lindsay, Chester, and I all shook our heads. Thrope wasn't kidding. "No plans to sell," said Dad. "*Still.*"

A decade earlier, our mom had been insistent we needed a bigger house. Mom hated the desert and our tiny, old bungalow home with only one bathroom. She was convinced a ginormous cookie-cutter house with central AC in a new subdivision would make everything better. That's how she met Thrope's former fiancé. He was the Canadian transplant Realtor with a fancy French-y kind of accent that Mom hired to sell our house and find her a bigger one. It turned out what Mom needed was not so much a new house, but a new life.

Our house was and is just the right size. In fact, it fit us all much better once Mom was gone. (We realized this after years of the family therapy that Dad made us go to.) Mom did finally find her big house—along with Thrope's ex, in a bitter cold North Atlantic climate we southwest desert kids could never acclimate to. Not like we really tried.

"Trying to kick us out of town, Ms. Thrope?" Lindsay said. "Subtle" is not a word that would ever be used to describe my sister.

"Yes!" Thrope said cheerfully as she unlocked her

Mercedes coupe. (And she would be the only teacher in the entire Rancho Soldado school system who could afford that level of swanky wheels. I guess it pays to not have your own kids but torture everyone else's, and be a part-time Realtor.) But before stepping into her Mercedes, Thrope looked at me and purposefully cupped her hand in the shape of the letter C. That was the grade she'd given me in her economics class, and it was probably a good part of the reason why I didn't get accepted to the Marshall School of Business at USC, my one and only college choice—and Thrope knew it.

Admittedly, I didn't do some of the homework assignments and yes, I occasionally skipped class (because a person can only take so much Thrope). I'm terrible at math, but put a dollar sign in front of a number, and I'm a star student. I aced Thrope's econ tests. I had an A-grade brain for economics, even if I had put in B-level effort. I deserved better than a C, and Thrope and I both knew it.

I considered raising a certain finger in response, but didn't. My hand clenched into a fist instead.

She ruined this town. She ruined my life. She needed to pay.

One final Cuddle Huddle in the school parking lot before we took a temporary break from BFF festivities and went off to celebration dinners with our individual families.

"We love you so much we might also go baldy," Slick and I told Fletch as we wrapped our arms around each other.

Fletch said, "I love you both so much I might steal you to Africa with me."

"I don't have a passport," whispered Slick, regretfully.

"I fear airplanes," I added. "But I love you so much I'll conquer that fear of being blasted through space in a disease container that defies the laws of the natural world."

"Do you even know the laws of the natural world?" Fletch asked me.

I shook my head.

"She'll learn," said Slick. "For you, Fletch."

"Break it up, you codependent freaks," a guy's voice drawled. I looked up and saw Jake Zavala-Kim, Slick's older brother and my brother Chester's best friend. Jake was forbidden fruit, and I was a low-class sucker for how badly I wanted to take a bite. Jake placed his hand on Fletch's bald head and started to rub. "Will this give me good luck?" he asked her, grinning.

Slick was not smiling. She shoved her brother's hand away from Fletch. "Don't flirt with my friends, asshole!"

"I wasn't flirting," said Jake. "I was *admiring*."

"Admire with *hands off*," Slick ordered him. Her mother used to reference a favorite old song and call her daughter "a slick chick on the mellow side," but when it came to this topic, Slick was anything but easygoing. She'd spent her entire middle and high school years having girls try to befriend her as a means to getting closer to Jake. As a result, she had serious trust issues, except for her Cuddle Huddle girls, obviously.

It was highly inconvenient that my hormones wanted to defy Slick's ban on Jake. My heart pounded hard—for how much I wanted to rip Jake's clothes off, and for what a lousy friend to Slick those lustful thoughts made me.

"But I feel huggy," Jake taunted Slick, as our fellow graduate Bo Tucker happened to be walking by. So Jake pulled Bo to his chest, but Bo literally flailed himself out of Jake's embrace, wailing "No hugs!" Most Likely to Be Hospitalized for OCD Germaphobia (and God Help That Hospital): Bo Tucker.

"I have a hug for you, Jake," cooed Amy Beckerman, coming up behind him. Junior year Homecoming Queen, Death Valley's disco roller-skating champion, Girl Most Likely to Start a Clothing Line for Strippers. Amy pressed herself against Jake, and Slick rolled her eyes, while I seethed. I wanted to be that press-on girl.

Lindsay, in the passenger seat of Dad's car, leaned over to the driver's side to honk the horn. She rolled down the window and shouted, "LET'S GO! I have a flight to catch." Lindsay had only come down from San Francisco for the day. We were on our way to Las Vegas for my graduation dinner, and then to return Lindsay to the airport there.

Fletch said, "Cuddle Huddle out. We'll resume operations tonight at nine p.m. Navarro homestead, as per usual."

"Good cuddle," I said.

"Good cuddle," Slick said.

Our usual good-bye complete, I stepped into the backseat of the Navarro-mobile and sat next to Chester, who was already asleep against the window.

Dad said, "I can't believe it's going to be just me and Chester at the house after next week."

Lindsay said, "I can't believe how sorry I am for you about that," while she simultaneously texted me in the backseat: I saw that side eye you gave Jake, dumbslut. Please don't tell me you're so common as to have a crush on the town man-tramp.

I texted back, There's a big difference between crush and lust.

Lindsay laughed and Dad said, "What's so funny?"

Lindsay said, "You and Chester having Friday night date nights eating frozen pizza and streaming Hugh Grant rom-coms once Vic has flown the coop. That's what's funny."

"I do love that Hugh Grant," said Dad.

I had no fucking idea who Hugh Grant was. But I felt a

twinge of regret at the thought of Dad and Chester bonding over him with a tub of popcorn, and without me there also. It sounded like quality dumbass fun.

Finally, my tears arrived. I started to cry in the backseat, realizing the enormity of graduation. I was leaving Rancho Soldado, the only place I'd ever lived. I was leaving my dad and my brother, and much more upsettingly, breaking free from my besties. Later on, after our family dinners, would be the Cuddle Huddle's last all-nighter together.

"What's wrong?" Dad asked, eyeing me with concern through his rearview mirror.

"Girl stuff," I said, so he'd stop asking.

Everything is over, I texted Lindsay.

Everything is just beginning, she texted back.

Lindsay turned around, reached over her seat, and slapped Chester awake. "Comfort your sister!" she demanded.

Chester patted my hand, and then went back to sleep.

I was not comforted.

I was not yet ready to let go.

6

THE MORNING AFTER
GRADUATION
Surprising Good News Despite the
Rudeness of a 10 a.m. Phone Call

"Make it stop!" Slick shrieked from somewhere deep in the barrel of her zippered sleeping bag as my phone's ringtone covered an old classic—Britney's "I'm Not a Girl, Not Yet a Woman." Slick hated morning light, which was why she'd closed the blinds and curtains in the basement the night before, making it impossible for me to locate my ringing phone in the dark cavern of our morning-after slumber party. Half-awake, I reached around the area surrounding my sleeping bag, but wherever my cell was, I couldn't feel it, or see it.

My forehead found it seconds later, thanks to Fletch

throwing it at me from the floor near her sleeping bag. "New ringtone?" Fletch asked.

"Lindsay," I mumbled. My sister had visited just long enough to attend my high school graduation festivities— and, I guessed, to mess with my phone settings.

"Dumbslut," Fletch whispered, reverently.

"All I need is time / a moment that is mine," my phone sang out.

"Make it stop already!" begged the blob beneath Slick's sleeping bag.

"Hello?" I whispered into the phone, standing up and walking over to the basement stairwell so I wouldn't disturb Slick. I didn't recognize the caller ID number, and I couldn't imagine who could possibly be calling me at ten in the morning. Anyone who knew me at all would be fully aware I'd be sleeping off the previous night's debauchery. And by "debauchery," I mean marathon late-night games of *Super Mario Bros.*, a jumbo Doritos pizza (exactly what it sounds like—an XL pizza with crushed Doritos as topping, no apologies), and infinite consumption of Oreos.

"Victoria? Is that you?" the voice on the other end of the phone call asked. Another thing anybody who really knows me already knows: Everyone calls me "Vic," except for two people, one whom I like, and the other whom I wish all kinds of evil on. I could tell by the old-lady voice on the other end of the line that this was the person I liked.

"Bev!" I said, concerned. "You okay? Do you need anything?"

"I need you to throw your fucking graduation party," Bev huffed into the phone. "What the fuck do I care?"

"No fucking way!" I whispered into the phone, honoring my cursing mentor the best way I knew how. She'd caved! "When?"

"Tonight."

"Tonight?" I repeated. "That's not enough time to organize and get the word out!" But I was already planning—decorations, food, music, and how to get the class to the party *without* Thrope sabotaging it.

"It'll have to be. I'm signing the sale papers tomorrow." Bev slurred her words, making me wonder if she'd had too many Bloody Marys this morning, which she confirmed when she took an audible sip from a drink and then exhaled, "Ahhh! Mary, don't you weep." She sniffled a little and then continued. "There're lots of RASmatazz pies and ice cream still in the freezer. Have fun, use it up, enjoy. You little Rancho Soldado High bastards deserve one last graduation party."

"What made you change your mind?" I asked Bev.

"I'm fickle. Just like you teenagers!" She laughed.

"And it would be an awesome fuck-you to Miss Ann Thrope," I added.

"That's just a bonus." It was a fair-handed slap to Thrope, who on the one hand had provided the buyers for Bev's real estate sale, but on the other hand was just an unrepentant fuckwad, which was how Bev typically referred to Thrope. Bev said, "Provided you can keep the unrepentant fuckwad from finding out about the party till after."

I said, "She's making such a fat-ass real estate commission, that oughta console her."

Bev said, "I'm serious, Victoria. She needs to find out *after* the party is *over*. That's your problem to figure out."

"I can handle it," I said with my typically misguided overconfidence.

"Promise me something," Bev slurred.

"Anything." I glanced over at my trying-to-sleep friends and couldn't wait to wake them the hell up with this amazing news. Last night's slumber party hadn't been our final hurrah after all! We had just over twenty-four hours till Fletch left for LAX for her journey to Africa. That was plenty of time to give us the best send-off in the history of Rancho Soldado: a final celebration in our favorite childhood place, Happies!

"Whatever happens tonight, NO ONE"—Bev shrieked

those last words, causing me to hold the phone back from my ear—"and I mean NO ONE, goes into the theme park."

"No one could go in even if they wanted to," I assured Bev.

"The ghosts of Ernesto and Mary Happie will curse you if you let anyone in!"

"I won't!" I promised.

I meant it. I'm hella scared of ghosts, just like everyone in our town. Rancho Soldado was built on the original gravesite of a battalion of United States Army gringos, who were killed in a minor but vicious battle during the Mexican-American War. The soldiers' campsite was ambushed by Native Americans, in cahoots with the Mexican Army, and their ghosts have been haunting the town that sprung up over their remains ever since, so we knew from paranormal activity.

And I would *never* risk being haunted by Ernesto and Mary Happie. For decades their small theme park adjacent to their restaurant was the only decent entertainment along the desert route between Los Angeles and Las Vegas. Then casinos came into neighboring areas, and business at Happies plummeted. After some scary gang fights in the park, Bev closed it down. It had been fenced and locked away for the past fifteen years.

"Promise me!" Bev repeated.

"I promise, Bev!" I didn't know why she cared that

much. No one I knew would ever even try to breach the twenty-foot fence around the theme park, mostly thanks to the hideous fifty-foot graffiti-covered clown head that hung over the park entrance. It was creepy as hell.

"There's no air-conditioning in the restaurant," Bev said, like she was trying to talk me out of the party she'd just authorized me to throw.

"No big deal. It'll be cooler at night, and we'll open the windows and run the ceiling fans."

The ancient AC system had been the final nail in Happies' coffin. When it died, the cost of replacing it was what finally made Bev decide to throw in the towel. You can't have a restaurant in a desert town with no air-conditioning.

"It's earthquake weather," Bev intoned. "Beware."

"There's no such thing," I reminded her. "We're more likely to get a brush fire in this drought than an earthquake." Generations of Southern Californians, accustomed to a mild and generally soothing climate, have created a myth that exceptionally hot, sweltering weather means an earthquake is coming. There's no scientific basis for "earthquake weather," but ask any native what the weather portends on a brutally hot day—even desert people, who are used to the heat—and they will say "Earthquake."

"The *Death Valley Psychic News* says we won't have rain again until Christmas," Bev said.

"Yeah, and the *Death Valley Psychic News* should know." I regretted my skeptic tone immediately. It would be mean of me to berate Bev's primary source of news, traffic, and weather when she was already so down in the dumps. I needed to perk her up. I changed my tone to upbeat. "You won't have to worry about drought anymore once you move to Florida, right, Bev?"

"Don't remind me. I'll just be trading in earthquakes and drought for hurricanes and humidity."

"I thought you were excited to move to Florida!"

"*Was.* Last night I found out my Florida boyfriend has another lady friend. She's called his wife."

"Damn!" For a second, I considered ditching the party plan and immediately jetting off to Florida to pummel whoever was responsible for breaking Bev Happie's heart. There was a special place in hell reserved for anyone who'd mess with Rancho Soldado's last surviving Happie. "I'm so sorry, Bev."

"Don't be. I disobeyed the primary rule of restaurant work. Don't fall for customers."

"I hear you," I said supportively, but shaking my head, as I'd already disobeyed another crucial rule of restaurant work: Don't fool around with coworkers while locked in the freezer room. Total Health Department violation. Then it hit me: Jake's Chug Bug! Tonight was the perfect night for its debut. He'd have a captive, and grateful, underage clientele for beer, he'd earn a ton of cash and exposure for his business, and he'd want to find a delicious way to show me his appreciation, so we could finish off what we started that time in the freezer room, and Slick would never need to know about the brief meetings of the body parts.

Bev said, "It will make me too sad to be there tonight, but you give Happies the graduation party send-off it deserves, and Thrope be damned. We had a fine tradition that should be upheld one last time. So enjoy those last pies. You're a darling, Victoria Navarro. A terrible, terrible waitress, but a champ." Bev was a whimper away from a full-on sob. There was nothing more I could say or do to console her. Happies was over. It was up to me to give it one last hurrah.

I wondered if, given her depressed, inebriated state, perhaps Bev wasn't in the best place to authorize me to throw this party. Did that obligate me to turn down this once-in-a-lifetime chance? Was I taking advantage of a grieving senior citizen? I considered that prospect for a millisecond and decided, fuck to the no. Even sober and not having found out her boyfriend was an adulterer, I knew Bev would want Happies to have a final good-bye party.

"*You* are the champ," I told Bev. "Thank you so much.

I won't let you down. I promise no one will get into the theme park, and the restaurant will be left in the same condition it was found, minus the ice cream and pies."

"I don't care if the restaurant's a mess. It's just going to be razed. But make sure the kids are cleared out by early morning. The lawyers are coming with the papers tomorrow at nine a.m."

"I will. Thanks, Bev. You're the greatest."

"Bloody Mary's the fucking greatest," said Bev, and I heard her down another gulp. "I'm not authorizing or condoning alcohol, by the way. But I recognize that kids will be kids at a party, so if you stupid shits are going to drink, there had better be designated drivers, or I will personally wring your neck. I'm holding you and you alone responsible."

"Got it."

"I left the key for you to open the restaurant under the mat at the back kitchen door. Knock yourselves out." She hung up.

PARTY TIME!

I stood up and threw a pillow onto Slick and Fletch to rouse them from sleep.

"Get up!" I said. "We're having a party tonight!"

"I hate parties," Fletch said. "That's why I hang out with you."

"Because you're too bossy to be fun," Slick said from beneath her sleeping bag.

"I'M FUN!" I yelled, more trying to convince myself than my friends.

I'm not that fun. I can be, but I have to, like, plan it. It's not a spontaneous thing.

In a week, I was leaving Rancho Soldado, probably for good. In my eighteen years of living in this podunk desert nowhere, I hadn't done a single thing for my town to remember me by, despite my many appearances at Town Council meetings with suggestions for improvements that Thrope made sure were never acted on.

That could all change tonight. We'd party like Thrope never existed. We'd pretend a version of Rancho Soldado could exist without her overlord tyranny.

Last Call at Happies, brought to you by Victoria Navarro, who will at least give her friends and classmates one final celebration to remember her by, and bring Annette Thrope's senior class party at Happies nightmares to fruition one last time.

CHAPTER

7   SHAMELESS MANIPULATION
    OF THE CUDDLE HUDDLE:
    IT GETS THE JOB DONE

10:15 a.m.

I called the Cuddle Huddle into session, joining my arms around Fletch and Slick for our usual circular team meeting. "I need a sick amount of help to pull off this party in such a short amount of time. Everybody in?"

Slick said, "I love you but I really don't want to help you if it involves heavy lifting or spending my afternoon doing anything besides napping." Slick was one of the dearest and clumsiest girls in the world; also one of the laziest. Not like that was a bad thing, but it was occasionally problematic. I'd already considered this variable and picked the perfect chore for her.

"I need you to set up the sound system tonight before the party. That leaves you the afternoon to nap, and to program the music. You can do it while you're swinging on your backyard hammock under the shade this afternoon. Dance music, no repeats, no EDM."

"A hammock afternoon not programming EDM does sound rather pleasant," Slick said.

Fletch advised Slick, "Maybe don't do it in the hammock. Because of . . . you know."

"I won't flip over!" said Slick. "I can sit with my laptop on my knees and totally program music and . . ." She paused, reconsidering. "Yeah, you're right. I'll do it on the chaise. Okay, Vic. I'm in."

I feared Slick would fall asleep too early this afternoon and then assign her little brother, Zeke, to her task at the last minute, but one trick to being an effective manager is you have to assign duties, trust they'll get done, and not micromanage every detail. I never worked at Happies long enough to advance from disinterested waitress to kick-ass manager who could put this principle into action, but I was fully aware of how to rally the troops. "Great," I said to Slick. "You're the best." I turned to Fletch. "I need you to—"

Surprisingly, Fletch slipped out from under my arm before I could finish. "Sorry, Vic," said Fletch. "Can't do it. I'm booked tonight."

"You just prematurely broke Cuddle Huddle!" Slick gasped, looking as betrayed as if Fletch had snatched the last slice of Doritos pizza directly from Slick's hand.

"Who cares?" said Fletch.

"I care!" said Slick. "It could be another year before we see you again! You can't just ignore our tradition at this vulnerable stage—"

"Fine," Fletch said. "We can cuddle huddle all morning if you want." She crouched back down to resume position, placing her arms around us. "But that doesn't change the fact that I have plans."

"To do what?" I demanded. Fletch had plans for her last night in Rancho that didn't include me and Slick? What the hell?

"My parents wanted to do something special," said Fletch. "So we're going dune riding at sunset once the heat cools off, and then driving to Vegas to get dinner at that amazing Thai place."

Fletch waited till *now* to spring this surprise on us? *I* needed her! *Don't freak out on Fletch*, I told myself. *Chill. Offer a compromise.* "Obviously you should go dune riding," I told Fletch, fully embracing the spirit of selflessness. "Great choice for your last day in the California desert."

Fletch rubbed her belly and performed a little hip swivel. She sang, "*I love my pad thai.*"

I smiled approvingly and let the moment linger without response. Then Slick jumped in. "Vic's too silent. She wants something." They both looked at me expectantly.

"Well," I said, looking at Fletch, "maybe you could go dune riding but please skip the Thai dinner part?"

"Toldja," said Slick.

Before Fletch could tell me why she had to go out to dinner with her parents, I hastened to add, "You'll end up driving an hour just to get caught in traffic on the Strip, and then you'll have to wait hours for a table because that Thai place—which makes you get sick half the time, despite you always saying it's worth it—doesn't take reservations. Do you really want that whole ordeal when you should be hanging with us?"

Slick took up my cause, and I hadn't even sent her a psychic request for support (because I felt it was implied). "Sad face," said Slick, pouting at Fletch.

Fletch looked appropriately guilty. "I know," said Fletch. "But my parents really want me to spend my last night here with them."

Now was the time for the hard sell. I said, "You're a teenager, Fletch. You break your parents' heart. *That's what we do.*"

"True," said Slick. "It's, like, our hormonal prerogative."

Exactly! We were so due this hormonal prerogative. None of us had been the types of teenagers who broke our parents' hearts by acting out and rebelling and all that. Slick's and my older siblings had blazed such a trail of naughty during their own teenage years that anything we might have tried would have been mere trifles in comparison. And only-child Fletch was too studious and serious to be bothered with the rite of teenage rebellion.

Slick's and my worst disappointment to our parents had been us deciding not to go to community college next year. Perfect-Fletch's worse disappointment to her parents was probably when she broke up with her boyfriend, Olivier Farkas, because she didn't want to be tied down to one guy any longer. They weren't upset that she'd broken up with Olivier so much as they were disappointed that the breakup got in the way of the prom photos they'd been waiting for years to place at the end of their "Genesis: Senior Year" photo album. Her parents had religiously organized yearly albums of almost every day of Fletch's life since coming to America, and the prom pictures were planned to be the culmination of that project before she left home for good.

I placed my hand beneath Fletch's chin and directed her gaze to the newly hung portrait on my family's basement wall, the remembrance that we had made to ensure Fletch's parents' prom photo dreams were still realized. With the words MÉNAGE À BFF painted at the top of the portrait, it was a large photo printed on canvas, showing

Fletch and her prom date(s)—me and Slick—dressed in atrocious bridesmaid gowns we'd bought for ten bucks total at the Goodwill store. In the picture, we were sledding down our favorite Mojave Desert sand dune spot, lying on our stomachs, our arms lifted in a V for Victory pose, laughing so hard that we fell off the sleds a second after the photo was snapped.

"I can't go to the party tonight," Fletch said, but with enough hesitation that I knew she could—and would.

"You can't *not* be there!" I said, aghast. "There is no party without you."

I could tell Fletch was about to break, but then her gaze narrowed on me. "This isn't about your war with Thrope, is it?"

"That's just a bonus," I said, repeating Bev's line.

Fletch shrugged. "A good one, I suppose. But I don't know . . . my parents will be so sad."

"Your mom will be relieved," I said. "You know how she loves to organize travel. Leave all the stuff you plan to bring to Africa on your bed this afternoon and tell her she can pack it for you tonight." *And then you can spend this afternoon helping me get ready for the party before I generously authorize you to go dune riding with the parents as a kind concession for them raising you so well and all.*

"Mom *would* love that," Fletch admitted, but still not officially getting on board. "And she'd probably be secretly relieved to have a few extra hours to double-check the passports and visas."

"Your parents have a lot they need to take care of tonight without the distraction of a jaunt to Vegas just for dinner," I told Fletch. Her parents were taking a month's leave from their jobs to join their daughter in volunteer work for the first month of her year abroad, so it wasn't like I was trying to take away their final hours with her. I was doing them a favor, actually, giving them this night back. I was probably saving the whole family from a post–Thai food, pre-transcontinental-flight diarrhea episode. Someone give *me* a fucking medal!

Still, Fletch did not budge.

I looked at Slick, sharing a moment of telepathy. We knew exactly how to close the deal. We started singing.

> *On the LA to Vegas*
> *hop hop hop*
> *Tummies ready for yummies*
> *At everyone's favorite dessert in the desert*
> *stop stop stop!*
> *Happies Happies Happies*
> *Super burgers then ice cream with a toy*
> *Where your happiness is our*
> *joy joy joy*
> *So come to Happies . . . hop hop hop!*

The Happies song and its hop hop hop dance were Fletch's number one favorites for life. The song had provided the gateway for her to learn English when she first came to Rancho Soldado. Learning the dance had helped ease her displacement anxiety. It was the first song Fletch ever sang, providing the introduction-to-America experience that she wrote about in her college essay that got her accepted to virtually every top-tier university in the country. Ivy League admissions coaches, take note: The secret to a great college essay is a weeper immigration story that ends with ice cream and a hopping song-and-dance routine at Happies.

By the end of the song, we were all hopping around my basement, an even better wake-up than Happies' super strong coffee sludge, and finally—finally!—Fletch said, "Okay! You broke me! I'm in!"

"Smart call, Ivy League," I commended Fletch. "Girls, prepare yourselves for the most epic going-away party of our lives."

I hopped back into the center of the room, where Fletch and Slick met me, and we resumed our Cuddle Huddle. Then we lifted our arms and high-fived each other.

"Good cuddle."

"Good cuddle."

"Good cuddle."

8 BEER SCHEMING

11 a.m.

I don't trifle with small-scale ideas, which was why I wasn't going to college next year, because I reached too high. (But whatever, USC Marshall School of Business. Me and my subpar GPA and SAT scores will have the last laugh when I make the cover of *Lady Entrepreneur* magazine without your degree and the ridiculous student debt that goes along with it.) If I wanted the Happies party to be big-scale fun, I needed something I was not old enough to legally acquire.

Beer. Beer makes a party big, and fun. It was also going to get Jake Zavala-Kim to show up, and if anyone knew where to find Jake, it would be Chester.

Having secured my best friends' help in the coming night's festivities, I bounded upstairs from the basement and found Chester sitting at the kitchen table, eating a bowl of Froot Loops. Not only has he not outgrown his childhood cereal, it's a daily necessity for him. It's like his Paleo Diet for Stoners.

"Are you and Jake working on the Chug Bug today?" I asked.

"Maybe," said Chester. "Or we'll work on the Mustang." Typically, he volunteered no further information. Getting my brother to speak more than a sentence or two at a time is a major chore. I think he has so little to say because Lindsay, Chester's twin, always did the talking for both of them. Can't get that girl to shut up.

"Is he in the garage now?"

As if she knew I was trying to press Chester for information at that moment, Lindsay texted me. Ask Chester if I left my favorite shirt in his car yesterday. I can't find it and he never answers my texts.

Chester shrugged in reply to my question and I didn't bother asking him Lindsay's; I'd just go check Chester's car later myself.

Jake and Chester spent their weekends fixing up the vintage automobiles they planned on converting into business endeavors. Jake's was the Chug Bug and Chester had a complementary venture in mind. With a vintage Mustang passed down to him from our dad, Chester planned to launch a late-night ride service called Drivers for Drunks. One of those ideas had a good chance to succeed; the other, maybe not so much. Guess which was which.

"Where's Dad?" I asked Chester. Usually the mornings after BFF weekend sleepovers, my dad could be found cheerfully fixing us scrambled eggs when we emerged from the basement hideout. Dad's scrambled eggs were often runny or overcooked so it's probably no coincidence Chester turned to cereal as his primary breakfast food. Even though Dad's eggs were less than stellar, my stomach grumbled for the comfort of them. They tasted like home. Ever since Mom had remarried Someone We Don't Like Who'd Once Been Engaged to Someone We Hated and then moved to Somewhere We Don't Like, North America, Dad was our sole provider, and cook. And with enough sriracha sauce thrown on, his breakfasts could taste pretty damn good.

Chester looked up from the cereal box he'd been intently reading while trying to ignore me. "Dad left for Vegas airport at the crack of dawn this morning. He got called back early to Phoenix."

For sure I'd miss Dad's weak chef skills this morning, but I wouldn't miss Dad being home, at least not this weekend! If Dad was gone, I had no argument over a curfew and no old person sniffing for beer breath when I got home. Happy Graduation *and* Merry Christmas, Vic Navarro!

I don't know why I paused, expecting Chester to fill in more details, but I did. When none were forthcoming, I said, "Why'd he get called back early?"

"Problem on-site that only he knows how to fix. Or so said the site manager. Stop interrogating me already."

For the past six months, since I'd turned eighteen, Dad had been commuting to Phoenix for a much-needed engineering consulting job. He worked there during the week and returned home most weekends. He'd taken a day off to come home early for my graduation.

"Hey, guess what?" I said to Chester.

"You're still here?" He sighed. I love my brother but man, I could not wait to live with my sister instead. At least she enjoyed my company instead of treating it like a chore.

I said, "I'm resurrecting the Happies senior class party. Tonight. Last time ever."

"Says who?" said Chester.

"Says Bev Happie. She personally authorized me to do it. Want to come help me?"

"I'd rather impale myself on Miss Ann Thrope's bayonet collection."

"Your loss."

"I'm working tonight, so don't ask me to bail you out of jail if Thrope finds out about the party."

"I'll ask Jake," I said, and turned around to leave the house in search of that very man.

As I was walking away, my phone buzzed. Lindsay again. Before I read the text, Chester called to me, "Tell your sister I put her stupid shirt on your dresser so you can take it to her in San Francisco next week. And to stop bothering me."

I sprinted out the back kitchen door, across the backyard, through the fence of trees separating our house from our neighbor's, and into the driveway of the Zavala-Kims' house. Fuck, it was hot out. I looked to the thermostat attached to the outer wall of the garage: 101 degrees already. I grew up with this hot, dry weather so it didn't faze me, but I did have a momentary panic, wondering how my party would survive in a restaurant with no AC. No big deal, I told myself. Enough ice cream and cold beers, and no one would care.

The garage door was lifted, and I saw that Jake's Chug Bug was parked there, next to his parents' food truck, Mexican Seoul, named in honor of the family's

Mexican-Korean heritage. Dad Jon (the Korean side) and Mom Selena (the Mexican side) drove their truck three plus hours each way to downtown LA to feed the lunchtime hordes on business days. Best kimchee chimichangas in the history of the world, according to online foodie reviews; personally, I was partial to their Korean BBQ–flavored tofu tacos.

The window blinds in Jake's apartment over the garage were down, so I assumed he was still asleep. I felt confident that when I explained the beer emergency and how he'd profit from it, he'd quickly forgive me for barging into his bachelor pad and prematurely waking him.

Selena stepped out of the back of the Mexican Seoul bus, looking like a punk-rock foodie goddess, with short black hair and deep red lipstick, a short black skirt exposing long, lean legs, a tight Mexican Seoul T-shirt, and black Doc Martens laced up past her ankles. She and Jon had Jake when they were barely out of high school, and then quickly added Slick and Zeke to their brood, and they operated their own food business while raising a family. For someone who could reasonably be expected to look haggard and exhausted, Selena managed to look like she hardly aged. Selena saw me and asked, "Where's my darling daughter, my darling Vic?"

"She's getting up now," I said. "She'll be home any

minute." Since Selena was in her work uniform, I assumed the Z-Ks had a job this weekend. I asked her, "Whatcha got going on tonight?"

"We're catering a wedding down in Newport Beach. It'll be a late night, so we'll park the truck at my sister's in Orange County and stay there rather than drive back to the desert after. Tell Mercedes she's on her own for dinner tonight."

YES YES YES! It was like all the parental planets were aligning in my favor, like beer destiny. Just because I love and worship Selena Zavala-Kim and she'd been like a second mom to me didn't mean I wouldn't take major advantage of her absence this weekend. It also didn't mean I wouldn't possibly be a bad friend to Slick by being a very bad girl with Jake Zavala-Kim.

"Jake home?" I asked Selena.

"Yah. I think I heard his snores from the open window over the Chug Bug."

Admiring the two business trucks parked side by side in the double garage below Jake's apartment, I said, "Won't it be great once the Chug Bug is operational? 'Cuz then maybe you and Jake could partner to cater local events."

"Oh, sweetie," said Selena. "I *wish*. I was there to support you at the Town Council meeting. I know you want local entrepreneurs to stay in Rancho, but there's just not enough business for us here. Believe me, I'd love not to commute to LA at five every weekday morning."

Jon emerged from the back door of their house and Selena tossed him a set of keys. "Ready to go, *mi amor*?"

"*Sí*, beautiful." He came over to us and placed a kiss on his wife's lips. It was weird how into each other they were for old people, and also weird how the fact of being so into each other made them not look so old. They were forty, but Selena looked like a rock star, and Jon funneled his manly good looks into occasional menswear modeling gigs. It was no wonder the Zavala-Kims' children were so gorgeous—at least Jake and Slick were. Their youngest, Zeke, was in that awkward teenage squirt stage, but every family has its runt, I suppose. Sometimes the runts end up being the best in the bunch.

Jon patted me affectionately on the back and said, "What's going on, General Navarro?"

I didn't want to lie to Slick's dad's disturbingly handsome face, so I figured not mentioning the party was the better approach. I shrugged and rubbed my eyes like I was still waking up and was just a typical teenager who'd goof off all weekend. Not that the Z-Ks would have minded about the party—they'd probably applaud it. But I decided it was better to say nothing for the time being.

"Let's hit the road before traffic picks up," Selena told

Jon. "Where's the kid? I thought he wanted to get dropped off for band practice."

"He's coming," said Jon. "Last-minute beauty preparations. You know."

Selena rolled her eyes. "I only have so much patience for his makeup routine. Let's back the truck onto the street now. If he's not outside by the time we're there, he can catch his own ride."

Zeke suddenly came charging out of the main house's back door. Diego Zavala-Kim, the baby of the family, aka "Little Z-K" and later anointed "Zeke" by his big brother, Jake, could officially no longer be considered little. The scrawny nuisance kid who'd spent the better part of his life trying to get me, Fletch, and Slick to interrupt our fun to play games with him, from Legos to Pokémon to *FIFA* to *Warcraft*, was suddenly over six feet tall and hulked out like a football player. He was wearing black "skinny" jeans that were too tight around his waist, exposing a sweet little roll of grabby chub below his wrinkled, also too-tight, purple Prince T-shirt, which had a picture of two doves crying on it. His side-shaved black hair with a rainbow flag–colored front pouf, and his big, puppy-dog brown eyes rimmed in goth black guyliner announced a semi-adorable, fully realized dork.

Zeke gasped at the heat. "Whoa! It's gonna be melt-your-dick-off hot today!"

Selena looked at the watch on her black wristband. "A scorching summer morning in the desert. Shocking. Ready to go?"

Zeke cocked his head to the side as he considered his mother's question. "I might need to reconsider this outfit."

Selena said, "Your fashion changes take too long and we can't wait on you, baby. Ask Jake or Mercedes to give you a ride."

Jon and Selena hopped into the Mexican Seoul truck and Jon turned on the ignition. As it backed out of the driveway, Selena called to Zeke, "And I've told you a million times. Liquid liner is much less likely to smear in the heat than pencil liner."

"I like the smear," said Zeke.

Jon placed his left hand out of the driver's side window, his pinky and index fingers extended as he waved in the metalhead death sign. "Rock on, Zeke!" Jon bellowed.

Zeke returned the metalhead sign. "I love you, Daddy!" he called to Jon.

The Mexican Seoul truck completed the distance out of the driveway, and was gone. The driveway gate closed and Zeke turned to me. "I heard you're throwing a party."

"How'd you hear so quickly?"

"Mercedes texted me to ask me to program the playlists."

Of course she did. No worries, I'd fill Slick's day with other tasks.

"Can my band play at the party?" Zeke asked me.

"Tonight?" I said. "You can't be serious." A newly minted *junior* thought I'd let his band play for the recently graduated *senior* class? Get a grip, kid. I had a reputation to uphold. Like I'd give over my party's vibe to some basement band of metalhead wannabes who probably invested more effort in their makeup application than developing their musical skills.

"I'm totally serious," said Zeke, but I ignored him and walked toward the door to Jake's upstairs garage apartment. Zeke followed me and inserted himself between me and the door, pressing his arm against the wall to block me. For the first time, I noticed his earlobes stretching down, holding wide silver earring tunnel rings.

"When did you do that?" I asked him, distracted.

"Do what? The hair? It's awesome, right?" He circled his head, proud to display the side shave and multicolored splash of hair in the middle.

I tugged on my own, nondeviated earlobe to show him what I meant.

"Oh, that?" Zeke smiled proudly and swung his head around again, perhaps to feel the breeze in the air holes blowing through his ears. "Why? Who cares?"

"I care. You shouldn't do that. It's unsanitary. Are

you auditioning for some Incubus gay cover band or something?"

"You're just jealous how hot I am now."

I chuckled. "Yeah, that's it, junior."

"So can we play or not?"

"Why do you want to play so badly tonight?"

Zeke said, "Because we need exposure. For future gigs. You'll have a captive audience there."

Ugh, there was no way this was a good idea, but I didn't want to be a big dick to this former little squirt. I needed to talk him out of it gently. "What's your band's name? Isn't it Hipster Trash? Because no one at my party will be into that kind of metal-goth music—"

"We're called Los Yunkeros now," Zeke interrupted.

"Los Yunkeros? What kind of fucking name is that?"

"It's Spanglish for junkyard workers. No hipster music. We've evolved beyond metal. We're, like, a punk-mariachi fusion band now."

I tried to keep a straight face. Didn't want to crush the boy and his punk-mariachi fusion band boyfriends. "No," I said, kind but firm. I was about to list all the reasons why I couldn't let Los Yunkeros perform—actually, there was only one reason, that I was 99 percent positive they'd suck, if the sounds I'd heard emanating from behind the Zavala-Kims' basement during Zeke's band rehearsals were any indication—when the window above Zeke's head raised.

"Children," said Jake, leaning out of the window. My heart fluttered and my knees went a little weak at the sight of Jake's morning stubble face and bare chest. I assumed (hoped) Jake was wearing his birthday suit below his exposed waist, but already his waking head was adorned with his omnipresent fedora.

"You woke up Daddy. Now please shut the fuck up so I can go back to sleep."

Jake punctuated his request by dumping water from a glass all over Zeke's head.

"You ruined my hair!" screeched Zeke. Indeed, the water bomb had deflated Zeke's polychromatic pompadour pouf.

"You're welcome," said Jake, laughing.

Zeke groaned loudly and then skulked to the back entrance of the main house. He lifted his middle finger to his brother, who in return gave him a military salute from the open window. Zeke slammed the door loudly behind him and disappeared to dry off and, probably, to immediately reapply product to re-elevate his middle swatch of hair.

Jake looked down at me. "What's going on, sexy?" he murmured.

"I've got a proposition for you," I said.

"I'll be right down," said Jake.

CHAPTER 9

JAKE ZAVALA-KIM:
BEER MASTER

11:15 a.m.

I didn't know why I was so hot for such a playboy. Really, I knew better. I guess Jake was the boy next door I'd been fantasizing about since I was thirteen, when I started to realize that boys could be used in ways other than how Lindsay and I used Chester—as a convenient punching bag, and someone to fix broken appliances.

I'd been with two guys since I was sixteen. The first, Troy Ferguson, had been my chem lab partner. One thing led to another in after-school study sessions and the grabbing and grinding that happened between practice quizzes was nice, but mostly, like, scientific study. (Dedicated students.) Awkward under the covers, not bad, but more an experience we wanted to get through quickly than get through skillfully (because we had no actual skills at that point). The second was my real skill teacher, Leandro de Araujo, the Brazilian exchange student I met at soccer camp last summer. "The Roar from Salvador," the other camp counselors called him. Leandro's love-making was very noisy, which I appreciated, because it made me feel appreciated. With him, I learned what delicious ecstasy could feel like. Raw. Carnal. Explosive. Slow, then quick, then sloooow, and sweeeet, quick again, BOOM, ohmygod wow. Leandro and I only had so much time to try as many positions as the Internet suggested before his student visa expired and he had to return to Salvador, Brazil. We used every minute most wisely. Honestly, though, I was kind of relieved when Leandro left because I was so exhausted.

Jake had almost become my third when we got locked in the freezer room at Happies. I hate jobs that don't get finished, and I was eager to put the skills Leandro had taught me to good use again.

While I waited for Jake to join me in the driveway, I walked over to his beer truck and admired how far it had come along. It now had a roof that lifted up, resembling a half-domed ceiling, so a tall guy like Jake could more comfortably stand upright in the vehicle when serving beer. The back of the bus had been recrafted with a new back door horizontally split in the middle; the top half lifted up and had customized leg pegs that could be extended to the ground to hold the door up, creating an overhead canopy, and the bottom half now had a custom-crafted countertop stored on the interior side that popped up from the floor and swung around to hang over the door to provide exterior counter space behind the bus. The whole vehicle had been painted a bright red with gold trim, and I knew the last and final stage would be black paint inside the CHUG BUG letters now outlined in black Sharpie along the sides of the bus. It was an engineering marvel, thanks to my dad's carefully drawn plans, and the handiwork that Chester, Jake, and Jon had put in every weekend over the past year.

I found it frustrating that Rancho Soldado was considered such a tumbleweed, nothing town. Just look at the ingenuity of its residents! Why did Rancho have to be a place that people felt they had to escape if they wanted to follow their dreams?

"It needs more," I heard Jake say as I was observing the masterwork of the Chug Bug's roof.

I turned to watch him approach the truck. His tall, lean body was clothed in a white beater top, slightly exposing his taut stomach and the beginnings of a happy trail that was otherwise covered by long panama shorts.

"What does?" I asked, wanting to yank the fedora

off his head and run my fingers through his mop top of scraggly black hair.

"The roof. I was going to install a chalkboard menu on it, but I'm not sure people would be able to see it clearly enough."

I said, "Can you put a flat-screen TV there? Then you could throw some beanbag chairs around the ground during serving times, and the whole area would be, like, the ultimate man cave. Add a server girl dressed in lederhosen with long braids and her boobs pushing out of her costume, park next to an artisanal Cheetos snack truck, and you've got a potential gold mine."

He grinned, and my skin felt warm and my heart tap-tappy. "That's not a bad idea, actually." His eyes moved down to my chest, which was covered in a barely there camisole top that I hadn't changed out of when I woke up. "Are you volunteering to be ale wench?"

"Give me twenty percent commission on all sales plus one hundred percent of the tip jar, and maybe." I wanted to tap myself on the shoulder in congratulations, for flirting with Jake while simultaneously discussing my most distracting sideline obsession: money, honey.

"I could only offer that generous of a profit share to a C cup. You're a . . . what?" Jake squinted, like he was peering more closely. "Solid B?" he teased.

"Depends on what time of the month," I joked. Jake

would have to work a lot harder to offend me by objecti-fying me. That was a sign he liked me, right? Like-liked me? Still, I crossed my arms over my chest awkwardly, not needing to further advertise that my cleavage got the same score as my GPA that didn't earn my admission to USC. *Average. Unspectacular. Whatever.* The thing about boobs that most straight guys don't get is that size is only part of the party. Volume is just as meaningful, along with the heart residing just below. Don't think I'm being deep, so to speak. That's a direct quote from Zeke, at the start of last summer when he counseled me to ditch the sports bra and buy a push-up one already. Always trust a gay with these fashion choices. Zeke was right; the push-up bra made a huge difference. It magically made volume appear, and my heart felt peace knowing the cleavage got more male appreciation, especially from the Roar from Salvador.

Jake removed my arms from my chest, and then leaned so close to my face that I could smell his minty toothpaste breath. (Nice, indeed.) "So what's your proposition?"

Now we could get to business and I would not swoon. I wouldn't. I said, "I'm throwing a party tonight. I need a Beer Master."

"Sorry, Vic. I have a card game in Vegas planned for tonight. I win enough, and I'll have the last seed money I need to launch the Chug Bug."

I'd anticipated his response, and had my superior pitch ready. "You can earn all that money at the party. *Guaranteed.*"

"How do you figure?" He sounded skeptical.

"Bev Happie just called to authorize me to throw a last senior class party at Happies. *Tonight.* The perfect audience for you to launch your beer business and get the word out!"

Jake whistled, impressed. Then he said, "Come on. You really think Thrope's gonna let that happen?"

"Thrope won't find out till it's over. I'll make sure of that. And what better payback for you to give Thrope than providing the beer at Rancho Soldado's last senior class party at Happies? I mean, its second last party."

Jake had been right alongside Chester digging that fateful well on Thrope's property back in the day. Paying for that damage was one of the reasons the two of them still lived at home. That, and they hadn't yet decided to spread their wings further. Why would they, when Sin City was just an hour's drive away? They could have all their fun there, and be back in their easy, comfy, air-conditioned, rent-free homes immediately after Vegas revelry.

Jake raised an eyebrow. "I'm intrigued by the prospect."

My loins might have experienced a tiny orgasm. Few topics make me hotter than commerce. And Jake talking about commerce? Epic hotness. But then Jake looked toward the barrels stored inside the Chug Bug and said, "But I don't see how it could work. I've only got three kegs. I can't have enough of my home brew ready by tonight."

"Nobody wants your craft beer, maestro. No offense. They want someone's older brother with a legal ID to buy cases of cheap beer, put them in ice, and sell it to them for a couple bucks a pop."

"Shame, 'cuz I could really use customer input on the stout I just crafted." Jake rubbed the scruff on his chin like a pensive professor. "It's got a chocolate aroma with a malt spine and subtle espresso finish. It would pair so well with Happies' ice cream and pie."

"Unless it's free, doubt you'd have many takers."

"I know. I wouldn't want to waste my craft beer on a bunch of dull-palate eighteen-year-olds, anyway. How many people ya got?"

"Three hundred fifty in our graduating class. I don't know how many people will show up."

"Do they know there will be beer for sale without watchdog ID checks?"

"Will there be?" I didn't want to tell people there would be beer if I couldn't guarantee it. Recipe for disaster.

"Which comes first, the chicken or the egg?"

"I don't know!" I said, starting to feel exasperated. This no-brainer proposition was taking him forever to accept. "Just answer the question. Are you in or aren't you?"

"I gotta figure out the math," said Jake. "Let's lowball, so . . . say you get two hundred people there. Of those, at least half will want beer. That's a hundred beers right there. Times at least two or three beers a head? We're talking a lot of beer. And that's a conservative estimate."

"If you can assure me there will be beer available, I'll ensure that prospective guests are aware."

"Then it's worth my effort," said Jake. "Gotta protect my investment. But here's the other problem. I don't have enough cash to buy that many cases up front."

I'd already factored in Jake's perpetual brokedness. Every dollar he earned he either put into the Chug Bug or gambled away on Vegas jaunts. "Your parents have a ton of cases they bought wholesale that are stored in the basement for the Mexican Seoul truck," I reminded him. "You'll make back enough to double their supply in return, like a thank-you note for a present they never wanted to give."

Jake shook his head. "They don't really care if you underage children occasionally drink a beer responsibly blah blah blah, but no way in hell they'll supply it for the whole Rancho senior class."

I shook my index finger. "*But!* They're staying in Orange County tonight at your aunt's house. You know your mom will want to take advantage of some beach time tomorrow morning, since they're already there. They won't be home till tomorrow evening at the earliest. That leaves you plenty of time to replenish their supply at Costco in the morning."

"I didn't realize you were so sneaky. I like it. I guess I *could* 'borrow' their supply."

"You're in?"

"I'm in!"

We high-fived. We were partners in crime now. Already I felt like a cooler, sexier person, someone like Selena. And like her, maybe I could also be a lover and a business partner to a Zavala-Kim male. It would be a temporary transaction, of course, because I was moving to San Francisco. But it would be a profitable fling on many levels, with dollar bills to boot on Jake's delectable booty.

"You're kind of a genius, General Navarro," said Jake. A minor, sensational tremor passed through the center of my body. Maybe this heat really was earthquake weather.

"Can you be set up at Happies by seven thirty tonight?" I asked.

Jake lifted his fedora with his hand, nodded at me, and returned the hat to his head, his signature gentleman's salute. I grinned. "Park in the back. There's no AC inside so buy lots of ice and make sure the brews are super cold."

"I will," said Jake. "This is going to be killer. Thanks for bringing me in. Maybe after the party, you and me.

We oughta, you know . . . count the money or something together."

"For sure," I said, trying to sound casual, when what I was thinking was, *OH HELL YES!* Great minds do think alike.

Jake leaned into me and I thought he was going to place a kiss on my cheek, but the soft touch landed directly on my lips—a quick sizzle of a kiss that promised more. Then he pulled back with all the casualness of that kiss having been a handshake and said, "You'll take care of Thrope? Because I can't handle that problem."

"Oh, I'll handle Thrope," I said confidently.

I had no idea whatsoever how to handle Thrope.

But I could figure that out later. For now, I walked away, offering a strut to my hips, hoping Jake was admiring my backside.

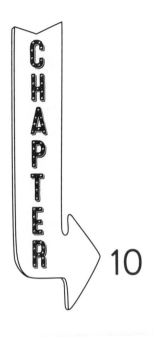

couldn't be more ready.

Pre-party Chores Accomplished:

✓ Invitations. The text message blast had been sent
   by Fletch, Rancho's outgoing senior class president,
   who had the master list of contact info. I had
   wanted the invite to say: *Last Call at Happies, final
   senior class party ever, tonight, 8 p.m. HELL YEAH
   THERE WILL BE BEER! SO KEEP IT FUCKING
   QUIET! You know why. Discretion . . . look it up!
   ALSO, BEER!* Fletch, more talented with manners

than me, successfully argued that we didn't want to offend our Christian and Muslim classmates with so many word bombs even if the cursing did honor our benefactress, Bev Happie, so the final invite said: Last Call at Happies, tonight, 8 p.m. Please with the Shhhh. No posting about it online. You know why, and it rhymes with hope. Senior class only, please. 🍺🍺🍺 Be a sport and travel in groups so there aren't too many cars parked outside the restaurant to arouse suspicion, and each carpool should choose a designated driver. Thanks, guys. See you tonight! (PS—once again, NO POSTING ONLINE!)

✓ Decorations. Dozens of strings of Christmas lights had been retrieved from my dad's outdoor work shed to provide festive lighting at Happies. I had easily sweated off all the previous night's pizza and Oreos in that outdoor furnace, but that would free up my stomach for Happies pie and cheap beer at the party. And an extra copy of the yearbook had been procured from over-extracurricular'd Fletch (yearbook editor, who had a whole box of extras), and then pictures from yearbook had been cut and made into decorations—streamers and wall flags—to hang around the restaurant for the party.

✓ Munchies. Best brownie recipe googled and sent to our class stoner, Jason Dunker, aka "the Dunk." (Frankly, I was amazed to learn he was a first-time baker in this category.)

✓ RSVPs. I had answered dozens of texts from classmates. `Yes, Emerson Luong, please feel free to contribute Jell-O shots. No, Jamila Beshara, parental permission slips are not required; in fact, they're discouraged. Remember the Shhh? Okay, Bo Tucker, you can bring gift bags filled with exactly five individually wrapped breath mints, a mini hand sanitizer bottle, condoms, and flyers for your OCD support group. Thanks, buddy!`

✓ Ice, Ice, Baby. Liquor store and hardware store run for ice and as many ice tubs for beer as the Chug Bug could fit was completed by Slick and Jake. Baby bro Zeke was authorized to come to the party even though he was a junior because he agreed to program the music and promised it wouldn't be sucky goth or electronic crap that only he liked. He was a Z-K. Of course he was in.

I was revved, stoked, pumped! I had one last errand to run before it was time to go to Happies to set up. And one more fucking piece of litter to pick up.

Standing outside Town Hall, I picked up a water bottle that somebody had left on the walkway, as if the recycling sorting bin to the left of the steps wasn't large and neon streetlight–colored enough and with clear black lettering to announce its purpose. Come on, people. Green for bottles and cans, yellow for paper, red for landfill waste. Easy! Obvious!

I placed the water bottle in the green bin and told myself it hadn't been a waste of my time to spend my entire sophomore year lobbying for recycling bins in public places. The Town Council had finally relented—mostly to get me to shut up, probably—but the bins were a visible sign that Thrope, who didn't want to spend the taxpayer dollars on waste reduction, was not unbeatable. (She preferred waste to be increased, by her very presence.) A good lesson to remember for tonight.

I was trusting the entire Rancho senior class to keep quiet about my party for just the next twelve hours. It could happen. Thrope could be subverted.

I couldn't wait for this party, and, just as importantly, I couldn't wait to rub it in her face after I'd pulled it off. *Tomorrow.*

Mayor Jerry emerged from Town Hall while I stood

on the outdoor stairs. He placed a key in the lock, saw me, and said, "Hey, Vic. Don't think I got a chance to congratulate you yesterday. Happy graduation!"

"Thanks, Mayor Jerry," I said. "You were great at commencement." He handed me a cigar. "You're a daddy!" I grabbed him in a hug.

He wiggled out of my embrace but grinned. "Congrats are premature. There are contractions but they're still spaced far apart. Doctor says if labor doesn't progress in the next few hours, she'll induce Darlene tonight."

"Amazing!" I said, feeling a full flush of joy not just for *him*, but for *me*. If Sheriff Cheryl's wife was in labor tonight, that was the best gift my party could receive. She wouldn't be available to field any nuisance calls from Thrope, should Thrope happen to find out about the party. "Good luck!"

"And good luck to you in Frisco," said Mayor Jerry.

"Nobody calls it Frisco. People from there call it the City."

"You're not from there, my dear Rancho Soldado native who regularly stalks Town Council meetings."

"I'll miss that."

"We'll sure miss you here. Who am I going to have bugging me about all those empty storefronts if you're not around?"

I looked toward the empty store windows lining Main Street on either side of Town Hall. "That's some prime real estate there just waiting to be revitalized," I reminded him. "It could be used to draw people to the city center to cultivate the local economy. People shouldn't have to go all the way out to the highway for goods and services when they could walk right here to Main Street."

Mayor Jerry glanced at the Rancho Soldado tourist brochures in my hand. The brochures displayed HAPPIES RESTAURANT on the cover and I'd just taken them from the information booth inside Town Hall. The brochures were outdated now, so what did it matter that I'd swiped the last remaining supply? These mementos of Rancho Soldado's last (and only) great institution would make perfect additions to Bo Tucker's gift bags, since he was going to the trouble of making them anyway.

"Shame about Happies," sighed Mayor Jerry. "Wish it hadn't had to end that way. But something good will come in its place."

"Something sucky will come, and you know it."

He chuckled. "That's all a matter of perspective. For you, it's doom. For others, it's opportunity."

We both noticed that Thrope—that very opportunity-maker—was walking in the center of the small park opposite Town Hall. Mayor Jerry quickly turned to me and said, "Good seeing you, Vic. I gotta go." He placed a baseball hat on his head and scurried out of sight, in the opposite direction of Thrope.

I totally understood. Normally I'd want to dodge Annette Thrope, too, but in this moment, I didn't. I had to know. Did she *know*?

I walked closer to where she was standing under the shade of the park's beloved old oak tree. The Realtor from hell was dressed classic Thrope, wearing an elegant, form-fitting, canary-yellow business suit, her butter-blond hair pulled back into a bun decorated with two red crossed chopsticks that could have doubled as her devil horns. She was with a group of older men and one young woman, my age. The men looked Chinese and were dressed in business suits, and I figured they were Thrope's real estate clients. I looked closer at the young woman. Was that . . . Bao Ling from fifth period Economics? What the hell was she doing there? School was out. Bao Ling already had a job lined up at a casino in nearby Vegas, so why was she still sucking up to Thrope? Bao Ling *better* not have said anything to Thrope about the party!

Wanting to look busy and not so blatantly eavesdroppy, I sat down on a bench under a tree and typed a text to my sister. Last Call at Happies party TONIGHT, courtesy of yours truly. I'd been so busy today I'd neglected to send Lindsay this all-important update.

I watched as Thrope pointed in the direction of the houses on the other side of the park. Thrope said, "As you can see, Rancho Soldado has a wonderful stock of charming mid-century bungalow and craftsman houses. These houses would cost millions in Los Angeles or San Francisco. Here, they're a bargain. They'll significantly increase in value once the new mall is built on the old Happies site. I suggest you start buying up now." Then Bao Ling translated what Thrope had just said to the businessmen, who all nodded appreciatively.

One of the businessmen asked a question in Chinese, and Bao Ling turned to Thrope to translate. "Does this park have a playground?"

"Oh, God no, not here," said Thrope. "There used to be one but we had it removed after a family tried to sue the city when a child burned his hands on a merry-go-round bar. You don't go to a playground in the desert at high noon! That's just common sense." She let out an evil chuckle. Patronizing bitch. "But don't worry. When the new subdivisions are built, the homeowners association will be free to build private playgrounds there. Properly shaded, of course!"

Thrope was the reason why young people couldn't wait to escape Rancho Soldado after graduation. This town of cool bungalow houses, which used to be a refuge for poor immigrants, beatniks, and people who just wanted big-city escape and a cheap slice of desert living, would soon be a bland suburb like all the others bleeding farther and farther outside the Vegas perimeter and closer to Rancho Soldado. My hate for Thrope was beyond personal. It was on behalf of all the residents of Rancho, whose town Thrope was ruining.

A businessman asked a question and Bao Ling translated. "How is the infrastructure here to support new business?"

Thrope beamed. "*Xiexie*, great question! We're working hard to modernize our laws to put business first. Tax benefits, environmental concessions. Rancho Soldado will be at the forefront of the New Economy. I'm not just a businesswoman and local politician. I'm an economics teacher, as well!"

Why would anybody be so proud to sound like such a manufactured scumbag politician, using big, sound bite–friendly words to offer false promises and say essentially nothing? When what she could have bragged about was how she relished in stifling innovation! She could have told the businessmen, *Delighted to report I spent the past year squashing the ideas of my recently graduated student Victoria Navarro! Since I'm the only economics teacher on the faculty, I was forced to be faculty advisor to the school's chapter of the American Teen Entrepreneur Club. Without any help or encouragement from me, Victoria took it upon herself to create her own plan for revitalizing Rancho Soldado as part of ATEC's annual business plan competition. She suggested that the town take better advantage of its location as a gateway to Las Vegas, the Mojave Desert, and the Kelso Dunes, as you'll probably see noted in our town's stupid fucking old brochures, because I stole that marketing language from Victoria. She proposed transforming the town into an ecotourism mecca, with the local small businesses going "green"—I know, big yawn, right?—and working in cooperation with one another to boost everybody. Ah, the innocence of children.* Beishang! *Yes, it* is *sad. What was that, how did Victoria's plan go over? Well, it would have gotten an F from me,* obviously, *but somehow her ignorant plan won the California state award, which led to her being invited to the Nationals competition. Fortunately, wiser heads prevailed at ATEC Nationals, and her plan lost to flashier entries from wealthier schools. But she's such a tenacious little badger, that Victoria. Just couldn't give up. She actually thought her plan was viable, and she dared to present it at the Town Council's monthly town meeting! Completely blindsided me! I mean, how foolish did that make me look? The town's economics teacher having no idea her own student intended to present an economic petition to the very Town Council on which the teacher so proudly served? Yes, yes, the Town Council completely dismissed her plan, of course. I made sure of that. [Sigh.] What can a teacher do? These idealistic children. It feels terrible to break their young spirits like that, but they eventually have to learn how the world really works, right? It's big business like yours that will revitalize places like Rancho Soldado. Out with the old, like Happies. In with the new: you! And hey, you do know I was actually a home ec teacher? Who was forced to teach economics when home ec was removed from the curriculum? Ha-ha, don't translate that last part, Bao Ling! 'Cuz I don't know shit about real economics!*

My blood boiled, remembering how Thrope had conclusively dismissed my ATEC plan at the Town Council meeting a few months earlier. But then I let out a loud laugh when I saw Lindsay's response to my text message. Hey, dumbslut. Don't throw a party just to impress a guy.

I typed back, AND give my girls the best last night together ever. But my laugh had been loud, and Thrope's group was staring at me as they neared my park bench perch.

I put my phone down as Thrope told them, "Soon I won't be an economics teacher anymore, though. I hope." For a second, as Bao Ling translated into Chinese, my heart leapt, feeling encouraged that future classes at Rancho Soldado High might be spared Thrope's tyranny. Thrope was finally ready to retire? Cue the parade! Thrope looked pointedly at me. Whatever she had to say next was personal between us, not her and them. She declared, "Because I plan to run for mayor this fall."

My heart felt like it stopped cold, I was so stunned. I'd thought demolishing Happies to make way for a mall and housing subdivisions was the worst fate that could befall Rancho Soldado. If Thrope became mayor—and of course she would win, no one ever contested her—then probably curfews and socioeconomic profiling and environmental apocalypse were coming next. Thank Bev that I was throwing this Last Call at Happies party, because it would probably be the last great thing to happen in Rancho.

I was mad, but maybe more sad. Rancho Soldado as I'd known it was dead.

I was confused, too. If Thrope really wanted to be mayor, she could have run years ago. "Why now?" I said aloud to the group.

Her tone typically condescending, she replied, "Because Rancho needs wisdom and experience to guide it. To make sure the post-Happies transition goes smoothly. Profitably, for those investing so generously in our town." Bao Ling translated, and then Thrope bowed to the businessmen, who bowed in return to her.

To the businessmen, I said, "Have fun homogenizing

our charming small town, destroying our environment, and stimulating growth with minimum wage jobs and housing no worker here could possibly afford."

Bao Ling started to translate but Thrope cut her off. "Shut up, Bao Ling." She then addressed me. "Don't worry, Victoria. I'll make sure Rancho evolves even bigger, brighter, better. *My* way. The *right* way. Your way is full of fantasy good intentions. Entirely implausible. You're graduated now. Time to deal in the real world." She walked by me without a backward glance, elegant and haughty.

I burned. I seethed. I silently promised myself I'd stay for the real estate closing the next morning at Happies just to show Thrope all the pictures of her former students defying her in her most hated place.

The businessmen passed me by, Bao Ling following behind them. *Does she know?* I mouthed to Bao Ling.

Bao Ling shook her head as she ran her index finger and thumb across her mouth. Her lips were sealed. Then she made fists with her hands and banged them down to her sides, as her previously impassive face turned bright with eagerness. Bao Ling leaned in to me and whisper-chanted, "Beer! Beer!"

Rancho Soldado would be forever ruined once Thrope became mayor. I grieved for my town as ardently as I couldn't wait to leave it. Drink up, kids!

11 DECREPIT IS THE NEW SEXY

7:30 p.m.

The desert at twilight at the end of a hot-as-fuck day.

I stood at the front entrance of Happies, trying to decide which spot was cooler, inside or outside. They were pretty equal parts sweaty, and I hoped anybody coming to the party knew about the AC situation (or lack thereof). I assured myself that with enough sugar and booze, no one would care how hot the restaurant was. Once the sun went fully down, the heat would downgrade from uncomfortably sweltering to passably awful.

Perspiration covered my body, yet I relished the hot, arid air of early twilight, my favorite time of day in the desert. When I moved to San Francisco, I'd miss this mystic window of desert dusk, when the air started to cool, and the vast, open sky was coated in quiet hues of peaches and apricots against a backdrop like a purple bruise.

I stepped back inside the restaurant, feeling excited about the night to come, but also aware of how much bigger this night was than just a party. Young adulthood was supposed to be about so many firsts—first crush, first love, first job—but everything tonight was about lasts. Last high school party. Last night with my girls. Last call at Happies. I didn't know what would become of us all in the future, but a moment of reverie for what Happies had meant to us seemed appropriate.

I couldn't remember a childhood birthday with Slick and Fletch that wasn't held here. The restaurant had been the preferred birthday party location of choice for generations of kids. It was a preserved relic of a bygone era that should have been a museum instead of slated for demolition. Ice cream cone–shaped light fixtures hung from the ceiling, with walls stenciled in swirls resembling caramel, hot fudge, and peanut butter sauce. Every door handle and window was fitted with custom knobs painted to look like pies. The ancient wood booths situated along the back wall were covered in years of etchings proclaiming customers' devotion to each other and to Happies. The wallpaper was ceiling-to-floor posters of decades of past Miss Happies, the beauty pageant once sponsored by the restaurant, and the beauties' pictures weren't just your usual white faces, but also Native American, African, Latina, and Asian ones. Happies was for everyone, and had been long before the Supreme Court dismantled segregation. The restaurant had an adjacent party room with a fake palm tree built almost as high as the ceiling and brightly colored piñatas dangling from every branch. The room included Skee-Ball games, an air hockey table, and its own custom *DDR* dance platform, covered in frenetic displays of the word HAPPIES, as if to stamp the word and its implications into every player's psyche.

With an hour to go until party time, I sat up on the cashier's desk situated just inside the restaurant's front, taking in the calm quiet before the party launched. I was the only person physically present, but all around me I could see the ghosts of past people moving about. I saw a table full of young kids celebrating, colorful cone hats on their heads, their spoons at the ready, as a team of waiters delivered a trough containing the Tower of Happies Power, Happies' legendary three-foot-tall pyramid of ice cream, hot sauces, whipped cream, and cherries. I saw a group of teenagers sitting at a corner booth, laughing and scanning the songs on their table's jukebox while they ate from plates full of burgers and fries. I saw a middle-aged couple returning to the site of their first date, rubbing their noses together affectionately between bites of RASmatazz pie. I saw weary travelers coming inside from the heat, awestruck by the displays of Miss Happies posters lining the walls, and salivating over the displays of pies in the cases behind the counter. I imagined Bev Happie as a little girl, sitting on her doting grandpa's lap at the cashier's desk, handing over change from the till to smiling customers.

I saw how happy this place had made so many people, and while my heart indeed panged with regret that Happies was all over, it also felt a surge of pride. My sleepy desert town created this wonder spot, and kept it alive for generations. So much had happened in this roadside attraction. Pageants had been won. Birthdays celebrated. Romances born. Major calories consumed.

I stared at the cash register, wishing I had the resources or even just cleverness to raise the money to buy Happies and save it from demolition. Probably USC had been right to deny me admission. I had ambition—but nothing to back it up. Who was the true dumbfuck in this town? Probably Victoria Navarro.

"Domestic disturbance at 504 Harrison. Can you take this one?"

The voice from nowhere caused me to jump off the counter in surprise. But there was no one in the room besides me. Then some static noises came from below the counter, and I realized Bev's police scanner was on.

"Roger that," said Deputy Sheriff Lane's voice.

"I owe ya," responded the first voice, which I realized belonged to Sheriff Cheryl. *"The wife's finally started serious contractions and I can't be going on nuisance calls right now."*

"Yes!" I cried aloud, to no one. I wished I'd remembered to bring the cigar that Mayor Jerry had gifted me. Now would be a great time to smoke it. I had hoped this would happen, and some unknown genie had granted my wish. Sheriff Cheryl's wife in labor tonight was the best news possible for the underage drinkers about to arrive at my party.

"En route to 504 Harrison. Good luck tonight," said Deputy Sheriff Lane.

"Good luck at 504 Harrison," said Sheriff Cheryl, laughing.

We're not such hicks in Rancho Soldado that we don't take a domestic disturbance threat seriously, but everyone knew who lived next door to 504 Harrison: Miss Ann Thrope. And she was known to call the police on her neighbors when their lovemaking got too screamy.

My Last Call at Happies could also double as my Last Laugh at Miss Ann Thrope, I thought, as I looked around the decorated party room. How Happies-hating Thrope would despise this scene! During the past couple weeks before Happies officially died, bored cashiers and serving staff had started making origami crafts out of Happies wrappers. Their efforts had not been in vain. Through-out the restaurant, strands of decorations made with their creations—Happies-emblazoned burger wrappers, fry containers, ice cream cone wraps, and napkins—were strung along the walls, side by side with the high school yearbook pictures I'd cut out and taped up that after-noon. The room looked like an art installation, I thought, silently patting myself on the back. And everything Thrope hated was celebrated in the party's decorations: Happies, her students, and carbs. Already it was the best party in the history of Rancho Soldado and it hadn't even happened yet.

I texted Slick: How's things going at 504 Harrison?

She replied: Screamy as ordered! I can even hear those horny apes over the music blasting out of their bedroom window. The chocolates, hand-cuffs, and '90s R&B mix CD Zeke put together worked exactly as planned. Go Team Cuddle Huddle! (+Zeke)

I wrote back: Did Thrope see you leave the care package on her neighbors' porch?

Slick: Doubt it. Zeke and I used the binocu-lars you gave us and saw Thrope through her window before we made the drop. She was at the back of the house on her computer.

Me: Do you think Thrope looks at porn?

Slick: Gun porn, probs. Uh-oh, Deputy Lane has just pulled up in front of Thrope's house! We're out of here. Will pick up Fletch and see you soon!

Me: Good work.

Slick: Thanks. Pause, then: Do you have any idea who ♫ Jodeci ♫ is and why they be feenin'? ☺

I smiled and put down my phone. I had no clue who Jodeci was and promised myself not to ask DJ Zeke, because he'd probably tell me, in detail, for about an hour.

Thrope was being kept busy. Excellent. I gazed at the restaurant's wallpaper, searching for Thrope's Miss Happies winner's poster, so I could give it the finger. Thrope's was the easiest one to find because it was so recognizable. Students at Rancho Soldado could often be found after Thrope's class looking at the image on their laptops or phones, trying to figure out how Thrope went from Miss Happie to Miss Ann Thrope. In the poster photo, Thrope wore a classic, museum-worthy aerobics outfit (spandex bodysuit with a Happies-emblazoned sweatband across her forehead) and had a rifle tucked into her Miss Happies winner's sash (she won the talent competition with her firing skills). The poster's text read: *Hello, Miss Happies Annette Thrope! Gorgeous Annette has got it all. This gal with the killer smile is the youngest Team Captain ever of the Rancho Soldado Rifle Club. She's also a California State silver medalist aerobics champion, and the mightiest poker player west of Las Vegas! Currently in her sophomore year at Cal State-Riverside, Annette plans to earn her teaching degree with honors, and we have no doubt she'll win that all-important Mrs. degree, too! Lasso this lady's heart, fellas, if you dare!*

Suck it, Thrope!

My stomach grumbled from hunger but it was still too hot to want much to eat. I scooped out some RASmatazz sorbet and took a lick. Perfect. As the refreshing sweetness glided down my throat, I made a mental note to self: *Ask Bev Happie for the RASmatazz recipes, trademark them, then market and sell RASmatazz pies, ice creams, and sorbets to the world; become rich.* Finally, I had a destiny beyond going to crash on the floor in my sister's group house in San Francisco till I figured out something better to do.

I heard a mewing sound from outside the back door and went to check it out, suspecting that the Happies' Cat Pack had come begging. A mangy black cat with big amber eyes greeted me from a cautious distance when I got outside. "Hold right there, little gremlin," I told the cat. Years earlier, when the theme park was still open, Happies let feral cats have free rein of the park at night, to keep rodent populations under control. Cat colonies still lived in the theme park on the other side of the fence, but occasionally drifters would appear behind the restaurant in the employee parking area. The cats knew they'd find sucker Happies employees who'd feed them, and, on particularly hot days like today, place ice bricks outside to help the cats stay cool.

Ever the sucker, I returned to the freezer room, took out a few bricks the staff had kept in there for the cats, and then stopped in the kitchen to retrieve a couple cans of tuna. I brought the ice bricks and the food outside to the back parking lot. "It's earthquake weather. Didn't you hear?" I said to the black cat. I placed the bricks at the base of the fence along with an opened can, and the black cat eagerly pressed against the cold bricks before moving on to the food bowl. I stayed on the ground to watch it, observing that the cats were entering and exiting the theme park through a small hole between the ground and the fence. I looked closer through the hole, trying to get a good glimpse of the park, but the view was too limited.

Jake's Chug Bug pulled into the lot, causing the cat to scurry under the fence and out of my sight. "Where should I park?" Jake called to me from the open driver's side window.

I stood up. "Right here." Jake parked the beermobile in front of my perch at the tall fence. "Mind if I climb up on your roof?" I asked Jake. The original VW bus's roof was still over the driver and front passenger sides of the vehicle; that part hadn't been sawed off in order to insert the customized section. It would make a great viewing perch.

Jake said, "I guess so. But what's that got to do with the party?" He put the Chug Bug in park and stepped out of it.

"Nothing," I said. "It's just for me. Help me up?" I lifted an ice brick from the ground to rub it along my hot arms, since the cat wasn't going to use it at this moment, while Jake stepped into the middle of the Chug Bug and raised the new part of the roof. I stepped inside the center of the Chug Bug, placed the ice brick down onto the old front part of the rooftop, which reached my neck level when I stood in the middle of the bus. Jake bent down slightly, and I grabbed on to his shoulder to steady myself. "Most girls would be all weird about letting a guy lift up her entire body weight," said Jake.

"Are you saying I'm fat?" I was not fat. I was normal-sized, but with a modest amount of Happies pudge that many employees acquired during work hours. When high school seniors who'd toiled at Happies graduated and went to college, their moving-away-from-home rite of passage was that they would typically lose the "freshman fifteen" instead of gaining it.

"No," said Jake. "I'm saying you're refreshingly unself-conscious." That was not true about me at all, but I suspected I'd just been given a small compliment. I liked it, and did not refute it. I placed my foot in his hands and lifted myself up onto the old rooftop over the front seats of the Chug Bug.

"What're you looking for up there?" Jake asked.

I stood tall and took in the view. "I was three when the theme park closed. I don't remember it. I want to see it before it's gone."

"Great idea. Help me up, too?" Jake said. Significantly taller than me, he easily hoisted himself up as I held his hands to assist him.

"Whoa," we both said at the same time as we gazed over the debris of the park.

"Don't copy me, Bill," I said.

"Don't copy *me*, Ted," Jake said.

We looked at one another and nodded. "Be excellent to each other," we both said, and laughed. I'm not too proud to admit that I knew practically every line from *Bill & Ted's Excellent Adventure*, but in my defense, that's because Jake and my brother Chester watched it, like, every day when they were adolescent boys. Actually, what's to defend? *Ace Ventura: Pet Detective* is my number-one favorite movie.

Thanks to Bill & Ted, I could totally appreciate a good time portal when I saw one, and Jake's and my view of the old Happies theme park was exactly that. An abandoned, decrepit little village, locked in time. Behind the enormous graffitied clown face was the area called Clown Town. It was a holding area with rusted lockers that had pieces sawed out of them and an information booth, in front of which there was a giant, rusted metal clown that had to be several stories tall, lying flat on the ground, facedown, as if hungover from a night of revelry. Beyond Clown Town was Main Street, lined on the right with a sign that said BYGONE RANCHO, and included a strip of fake Western mining town building facades—a general store, a bank, a saloon. On the left was a sign for the UnHappies Jail, which had been the last stop for drunk or contentious park visitors before they got kicked back to the security team in Clown Town and then sent on their way out of the park. The remnants of the UnHappies Jail structure were mostly still there. It had standing walls at the sides and at the back, with jail cell bars still in the ground in the front, but no ceiling. Bottles and cans and random cactus trees sprouted up in the middle. In the farther distance past Main Street, a merry-go-round of fallen horses lay with weeds sprung up between them, and there was an entire field of faded and picked-apart bumper cars on their sides.

The park was a mess, but there was something beautiful about it, too: a time capsule that Mother Nature had taken back. The sight was haunting and creepy, but also breathtaking. I would have pulled my phone out to take a picture, but somehow I sensed the park didn't want to be photographed. It wanted to be left as is, not captured in an artificial image that didn't breathe and swelter in its natural desert habitat.

Maybe the sight made Jake as pensive as it did me. "I was conceived in that park," Jake noted.

"No way."

"True story. In Lovers Lane." Jake pointed to a weeded-over miniature golf course in the distance, past Main Street, where you could still see the heart-shaped "Lovers Lane" castle at one of the tees. I knew Selena and Jon Zavala-Kim had once been scandalous prom royalty—a pregnant prom queen and her baby daddy prom king—who married right after graduation, but I had no idea their courtship spawned inside Happies' ancient Lovers Lane castle.

"Impressive," I said. "I'm surprised they fit in there. It doesn't look that tall."

"I think the horizontal ratio was more important than the height," said Jake, laughing. Then his face turned more serious. "You're cool, you know that? It wouldn't even have occurred to me to take in one last view. But you, like, see the big picture of things. When all this is gone, I'm gonna be glad to have this last image in my head of what old Happies looked like in its final hours. Like, maybe the most beautiful place I've ever seen."

Whoa, as Bill & Ted would have said. "I'm not cool," I

said. "Actually, I'm hot as hell," meaning that literally. My skin burned as beads of sweat rolled down my back.

"Yeah ya are," said Jake, and my heart dipped like a soft-serve cone in hot fudge sauce.

Suddenly, I was soothed. Jake lifted the ice brick I'd left on the roof and rubbed it down the back of my neck and then along my spine. "That feels nice," I said.

"I'll rub your back if you'll rub mine."

I smiled and held my hand out. He placed the cool brick into my hand, and I returned to rub down his perfect spine, and his hips swayed happily.

Flash memory: half an hour after closing time at Happies. We were in the freezer room to do an inventory check for the next day's supply order. The door jammed, again, because Bev never wanted to pay the money to have a new one custom-made. "Paco knows how to fix it," I assured Jake. "He used to be a locksmith before he became the cook here."

"After his brief incarceration for unlawful entry into some rich folks' homes to steal jewelry," Jake said, laughing. "Yeah, we can trust that guy to help us out."

"Rumor. Not confirmed," I said.

We pounded our fists against the door until we heard longtime waitress Missy's voice from the other side. "Paco's on break. He rode over to Al's Wine 'n' Donuts for some smokes. He oughta be back in ten. Hold on in there, shouldn't be long." She snort-laughed. "I'm sure you kids can think up ways to stay warm till Paco gets back."

Jake raised an eyebrow at me. "We gotta pass some time," he said. "Nobody disobeys Missy if they wanna be let back into Happies." I raised an eyebrow in return. Was he actually propositioning me after all these years I'd been secretly crushing on him? Did he just not care about Slick's rules?

"That's true," I whispered. I'd never disobey Missy. I regretted that I would disobey Slick. Her brother was too irresistible. Slick never needed to know.

Jake stood before me, like inches away, smiling. "Yeah?" he whispered. "Yeah," I said. He moved closer until he pressed into me and my back slid against the cold door. My skin didn't have time to process the chill because immediately Jake's lips were on mine, and oh wow, his tasted like mint chocolate chip ice cream, and I couldn't wait to discover how the rest of his flesh tasted.

Then Paco the cockblocksmith returned from break, way too early.

Now, on top of the Chug Bug, once again I felt the same warm sensation spreading across my body as I felt during that freezer room lock-in with Jake. I rubbed the ice brick along Jake's back, thinking about what we'd be rubbing later, when we were counting the money. "Mmmm," Jake said.

"Mmmm-hmmm," I said.

Yes, we produce well-rounded, eloquent scholars here in Rancho Soldado.

The blast of a loud song ended the moment. I threw the brick onto the ground, as Fletch and Slick waved their arms out of Selena Zavala-Kim's SUV windows and Gwen Stefani sang from the speakers, *"Hey baby, hey baby . . ."*

"Hey!" we all three cried out.

Jake looked at his baby brother, Zeke, in the driver's seat. "The Cuddle Huddle is called to session," Jake said, imitating what Slick, Fletch, and I would say when we were ditching others' company for our own company. Jake jumped back down into the Chug Bug while Zeke screeched, "Par-tay!"

The Chug Bug roof height wasn't too high, so I jubilantly jumped down to the ground to greet my girls. "Showtime!" I squealed.

Slick and Fletch got out of the Z-K car while Zeke head-thrashed in the driver's seat in time to the song on the stereo. We girls formed into Cuddle Huddle, joined our fists in the middle, then lifted our arms in unison. "Good cuddle!"

Once disbanded from the Cuddle Huddle, Slick said to Jake, "We've got a shitload of ice in the back of the SUV. Can you unload it into the Chug Bug 'cuz I don't feel like it."

"I bought you a six-pack of Guinness," Jake said, who

knew how to play Slick even better than me. He tossed her a warm can. She liked her beer cold, but her beloved Guinness cans warm, as they're supposed to be. Just because we live in the desert doesn't mean we're savages.

"Sucker punched again," said Slick. She popped open the can and took a gulp. "Ahhh! Okay, I'll move the ice to the Chug Bug. Come on, Zeke. You help me."

I looked at Fletch. "Help me with the ice cream?"

"Yep," said Fletch.

The two of us headed toward the Happies back door as Slick called to us from the Chug Bug. "I love you so much the moon farts snowflakes."

I called back, "We love you so much we'd even slay Bambi's mom if she got all up in your shit."

Fletch said, "We love you so much that afterward we'd take you with us in our murder-suicide pact 'cuz we're so distraught for being such fuckheads who'd kill Bambi's mother."

"Aw, you guys are the best," said Slick. "I love you so fucking much."

"SHUT UP!" the brothers Z-K said.

As Fletch and I entered the restaurant, she cried out, "Crap! It might be hotter in here than it is outside."

"Think people will bail?" I asked. "That is, if they even show up?"

"They're natives, they know what to expect," said Fletch. "Of course they'll show up. But where are those ice bricks? My *caliente* arms need some of that sexy action *now.*" She winked at me and I stopped walking. Wait. What did she know? She leaned closer to me, confidentially. She said, "So, have you sampled Jake yet?"

I was about to defensively announce *No! I would never do that with Slick's brother!*

But then Fletch said, "Because I have, and just between us, you absolutely need to tap that at least once before you leave."

12 DECEITFUL DUMBSLUTS

7:45 p.m.

Fletch and I stood in the long hallway between the restaurant and back parking lot, facing the bathrooms. The news was too urgent. I couldn't even wait to drag her farther inside for a proper sit-down gabfest over a piece of Happies RASmatazz pie in our favorite booth.

"Does Slick know?" I asked, whispering, even though Slick couldn't possibly hear us in the back parking lot over Zeke's car stereo disco music, and Zeke loudly singing, *"I'm your boogie man! That's what I am!"*

Fletch said, "Does she know what? That you like Jake, or that I've been with him?"

"Both."

"Of course not! She'd freak."

I didn't know which was harder to comprehend: that Fletch had been with Jake, or that my thing for him was so transparent. "Is it that obvious?" I asked, mortified.

"No. You play it cool. I really didn't have a clue until I just saw you two up on top of the Chug Bug."

I grabbed her arm in concern. "Do we suck because we lust after our best friend's brother?"

Fletch said, "We're deceitful dumbsluts. I admit it! But we don't suck. Look at him." We glanced down the hallway outside to Jake, whose modest mountains of biceps were on display as he lugged bags of ice into the Chug Bug, whose core muscles were so strong that he could effortlessly lift heavy loads and still the fedora never dropped from his head. Whatta guy. Fletch and I both let out quiet but appreciative catcall whistles. She said, "Let's sit down now, because I plan to dance the rest of the night away." Fletch took my hand from her arm and led me inside the restaurant. We sat down at the corner table where we'd spent the greatest percentage of our collective Happies time together—talking, eating, laughing, snarfing. Our butt shapes were practically imprinted into the seat covers in this booth. Again, my heart ached. This would be the last time ever that Fletch and I shared this booth.

I said, "So what happened between you two? And how did you not tell me before now?"

"I don't tell you *every*thing," said Fletch.

"You should." Did I have to state the obvious?

"I tell you 99.9 percent of everything. This felt like a .1 percent to keep to myself."

I started tallying in my head and said, "Maybe it's more like 5 percent? Because you also didn't tell me you'd deferred Yale until a week after you'd decided. You didn't tell us you'd broken up with Olivier until just before prom. Why didn't you say anything about Jake?" Fletch was about to go off and live a whole other life I wouldn't be privy to except in Skype chats and occasional holiday visits. It concerned me that she was already withholding so much crucial information.

Fletch said, "I was worried you'd be mad at me on behalf of Slick."

"Give me more credit. I can compartmentalize, at least where Jake is concerned! Do you still have a thing for him?" It was bad enough to wish to do scandalous things with my best friend's brother. It would be worse to wish it with my other best friend's secret tryst partner.

"Had. It was a passing curiosity."

"Since when?"

"I guess it started when we were in middle school and Lindsay's friends were always going on about him being the hottest guy in school and how every girl wanted to get with him because he had such specific talents. I always wanted to know *which* talents. Remember?"

"Of course I remember. Listening in on Lindsay's friends had the same effect on me! How did we never discuss this together before?"

Fletch didn't answer that question, because we both knew why: Slick. Fletch asked, "Lindsay never experimented with Jake? Not even just to be sure she wasn't into guys?"

Instinctively, I took out my phone to text Lindsay, and then I set it down, knowing better. "No way. Jake is Lindsay's twin's best friend. Lindsay actually has a sense of family ethics, which apparently I didn't get." I leaned closer to Fletch and revealed, "But Lindsay did tell me she once gave Jake a private birthday gift of lesbian porn made by and for women. So he'd learn proper techniques."

Fletch took my hands in hers from across the table and gave them a sincere squeeze. "Your sister is a great dumbslut. That was probably the best community service outreach effort she could ever make for the eligible female population of Rancho Soldado."

I said, "I thought Olivier was the only guy you'd been with." I felt weirdly disappointed. *Every* girl liked Jake, and Fletch was not every girl. She was Rancho Soldado's number one everything. She was the one who always rose above. Fletch was better than the rest of us, and the rest of us were okay with that, even comforted by it.

Fletch said, "Your face right now is why I didn't tell you. You don't look betrayed; you look let down. Like once again I haven't lived up to your image of me."

"Once again?" I said, regretting that my face so clearly indicated my feelings. "When have I ever said you didn't live up to my image of you?"

"It's not something you say so much as what I feel is implied. 'Fletch is the smart one.' 'Fletch is so responsible.' 'Fletch, don't waste your time on a frivolous gap year in Europe when you could be doing volunteer service helping the world!' That's a lot of pressure. I hate that sometimes you guys make me feel like, 'Fletch never fucks up like everyone else.'"

I thought: *You're right, you don't fuck up. Except this one time.* Fletch hadn't fucked up because she fooled around with Jake, in my opinion. She fucked up because she kept it from me, and assumed I would judge her if she told me. And that's exactly why she was the smart one. I *was* judging her. It stung she felt that way about me, but bruised deeper that she was right to feel that way about me. "I think you're awesome and indomitable," I said. "What's wrong with that?"

"Nothing. It's appreciated. Sometimes I just want to feel normal. Mortal."

I laughed. Genesis Fletcher, a mere mortal? Ha! I didn't know how to acknowledge that she could be anything other than invincible, so I steered the conversation back to anyone's favorite topic after money and what's for dinner: sex. I said, "So you and Jake: When? You only broke up with Olivier in April."

"It was beginning of last summer, when you were away at soccer camp and Slick was visiting her aunt. When Olivier and I broke up the first time. It was just a weekend fling. There was a lot of tequila involved. Not a big deal."

It was so a big deal, and she knew it, otherwise she would have told me right after it happened. I said, "What was it like with Jake? It couldn't have been that great if you just got back together with Olivier a few months later."

"One had nothing to do with the other. See, I can compartmentalize, too." She paused and looked at me with concern. "You know to keep it casual with Jake, right? I don't want you to get hurt. Jake's a player, not a boyfriend."

"I know that," I said, probably too quickly. Then, I admitted, "I'm so relieved to be able to talk about him."

"I know. It felt wrong not to tell you, but I didn't want to risk Slick getting upset. She hates hearing about his conquests. But she needs to accept that lots of females around here have their way with her hot brother."

"Slick accepts it. She just couldn't deal with it if you or I were concerned."

Fletch said, "I don't have siblings, so I don't really get why she cares so much. Would you be pissed if Chester hooked up with me?"

I couldn't answer the question because I was laughing too hard. "Chester *wishes*!" I finally said between convulsive fits of hysteria. The idea of Chester being able to score a girl who was both brilliant and beautiful implied that he had the verbal capacity to even start a conversation with one. He barely talked to *me*, and I'd lived in the same house with him for eighteen years. He shared a womb with Lindsay, and still couldn't be bothered to return her phone calls or texts. I worried a lot about my brother and hoped he wasn't destined to be a middle-aged bachelor still living in our dad's house, collecting cereal boxes for entertainment. Should I drag Chester to San Francisco with me, kicking and screaming, just to be sure he finally took a chance and lived somewhere else in his life? *Lived* his life, rather than just sit around waiting for it to happen in between his shifts at Al's Wine 'n' Donuts?

Once I calmed down from the laughter, I said, "You know why it's such a big deal to Slick. She hates feeling that people in this town—especially girls—like her to get to him."

"But we liked her first," Fletch pointed out.

I shrugged. "Somehow I don't think that's gonna matter."

"So we'll just keep the Jake indiscretions to ourselves," said Fletch.

"Does that make us bad friends?"

"We're *great* friends," said Fletch. "Exactly because we keep the indiscretions to ourselves and don't bother our dear Mercedes Sabrina Zavala-Kim with insufferable information about her brother that's of a highly erotic nature."

"It was erotic with Jake?" I honestly wanted to stop time and hear every detail Fletch was willing to share. As a preview for what I could hope for—and the standard I would strive to uphold.

"Yeah. But mostly I just wanted to use the word 'erotic.'"

"How did it feel?"

"The hookup with Jake, or using the word 'erotic'?"

"Both."

Fletch stood up and performed a hips-thrusting dance. "Fucking *awesome*."

The details were in her dance. I laughed even while my heart winced, as I understood just how much I was going to miss Genesis Fletcher. I knew I'd love living with my sister and I'd love San Francisco, but, for the first time,

I understood that there would be actual physical pain in my heart involved once Slick and Fletch and I were living far apart.

There's always time for pie.

The party was about to start and I surely had more important things to do, but I went to the pie case and cut a slice of RASmatazz for Fletch and me to share as she walked around the restaurant, admiring the party decorations.

She said, "The origami wrapper art is a stroke of genius. And while I don't love that you wasted one of my precious yearbooks that I killed myself getting budgeted to produce, I do love the cut-up pages and pics on the walls. The place looks amazing. Great job, General Navarro."

I said, "Sometimes when I reach beyond my grasp, I astound even myself."

Fletch said, "Yeah, tell that to Arizona State and UNLV, where you should have also applied. Because you would have gotten in." She came over to the cashier's counter where I'd brought the pie and pointed to the windows facing the front parking lot. The windows were now covered in cardboard, like a hurricane preparation tactic. Fletch pointed to the cardboard and asked, "And this is festive how?"

I said, "The cardboard's there so it's not so obvious to cars whizzing by that a party's happening inside." I looked through the peephole in the cardboard that I'd cut out at eye level so I could monitor incoming traffic in the front parking lot. So far, no cars were arriving. I took a bite of pie, and Fletch did the same. "And I'm not worried about stupid colleges. But I am starting to worry about food. There's not enough here."

Fletch glanced toward the pie case. "Looks to me like you've got enough pie. The Make-Out Your Own Sundae Bar in the *DDR* room is fully stocked. The Chug Bug's here. What's your worry?"

"There's no real food besides ice cream and pies to feed the masses. People will need something more substantial in their bellies to stave off extreme drunkenness later tonight. I've been so busy arranging the beer and party decorations, and how to thwart Thrope, that I didn't plan well for food besides the leftovers already here at Happies. I should have arranged food for taco'clock, when the party's ending and people will need it most."

One in the morning was taco'clock in Rancho Soldado. On blazing-hot summer nights, the town's insomniacs had a long-standing tradition of sharing taco meals on the front porches of their bungalow houses. Take a little bit of carne asada or fish or potatoes, some fresh guac, throw on some Cotija cheese, and add cold beer and some good folk to help pass the time, and all the problems of the world could be solved—or at least forgotten—under the starry skies.

"Is taco'clock really a thing?" Fletch asked. "Because I've lived in this town since I was five, and I've yet to experience it."

"That's because you live in the newer part of town where people's big houses are fenced off and not that close together."

"So it's not just one of your Rancho myths?"

"I have Rancho myths?"

"Maybe 'myths' is the wrong word. You idealize Rancho to make it this place you want it to be rather than the kind of dump it often is. Sorry, honey. I know you don't like to hear it. I mean, who else but you would bombard the Town Council with a twenty-five-page report about how to modernize the infrastructure and grow the local economy through sustainability platforms rather than pure profit incentives? It was a brilliant plan. Don't get me wrong. I'm just saying no one else in this town could be bothered that much to care. It's sad, actually. Taco'clock shouldn't be a myth that only you and maybe twelve other people practice. It should be law."

"It *is* sad," I said, starting to feel morose before what could be the most exciting night of my life so far. It was like Fletch was implying I should be embarrassed to be so invested in my hometown. Even if it was a nothing place in the middle of nowhere, its most notable distinction being a now-defunct restaurant located just off the road to somewhere (else), and that some of its residents had an excellent but vague tradition of celebrating taco'clock in the middle of the night, that didn't mean I couldn't love it.

"Don't get all offended, Vic," said Fletch. "I'm just saying this town's too good for you. I'm glad you're leaving. If no one here cares about it other than you—except maybe Miss Ann Thrope—it's hella time to go."

Through the cardboard peephole, I saw lights of cars and trucks pulling into the front parking lot. People were starting to arrive. The name "Thrope" made me nauseous with anxiety. I put my fork down.

"Showtime!" I said weakly. Worse than Thrope finding out was the fear: What if my party bombed?

"One more thing to do." Fletch reached into her purse for her makeup bag, and looked into the mirror on the wall at the cashier's counter. She applied a coat of burgundy lipstick to her full lips, the only makeup on her dark, angular face. She said, "I'd put on mascara but what if we're all crybaby by the end of tonight?"

"I wouldn't bother with mascara unless it's waterproof. With this heat, you'll sweat it off before you can cry it off." I licked my index finger and then dabbed it beneath my eyelids to remove the mascara that had already smudged there only minutes after applying it. My forehead was sweaty and my shoulder-length dark brown hair was sticking to the back of my neck from the heat. I asked Fletch, "Do you have a headband or something that I could borrow to hold my hair back?"

She rubbed her hands over her closely shaved head. "Sorry. I gave those up when I went baldy. Not having hair is *great*. I highly recommend."

"I miss your braids."

"Grow your own," said Fletch, patting my back comfortingly as I stood next to her, observing our reflections in the mirror. "Unless you want to chop yours off and go to Africa in my place so I can use all the money I saved working here to backpack across Europe instead. Your pale self will fry even faster in the sub-Sahara than it does here."

I looked in the mirror. My face was a melting pot of ethnicities—my Irish-American grandmother's blue eyes, my Native American grandfather's dark brown hair, my Filipino grandfather's nose—but my Polish grandmother's fair skin was indeed not suited for the desert. Soon it would be in a more suitable habitat: foggy San Francisco.

I sniffed, thinking I smelled smoke. Automatically, my eyes shot toward the cook's station behind the pie counter, but of course there was no one in there, and I knew the gas for the stove had been turned off when Bev closed the business. My head turned the other way, to the peephole. Through it, I saw the first set of party arrivals—a group of girls standing in the back of a pickup truck, while on the ground below them, a semicircle of guys appeared to be trying to light up a charcoal grill someone must have brought with them.

This was a graduation party, and *not* a tailgate party! Festivities hadn't even begun and already these numbskulls were poised to flare smoke signals to alert the authorities. I ran outside.

13

THROW A BARBIE ON THE BARBIE

8:30 p.m.

"Finally! Tonight's the night we throw a Barbie on the barbie!"

Standing in the bed of Jason Dunker's pickup truck, Slick held up a naked Barbie in her hand as Jason lit up the coals in his charcoal grill with a *whoosh* of flames. It wasn't just any Barbie, but the one we had most tortured in our childhoods. We called her Ugly Stepchild Barbie, and over the years, this Barbie's luxurious blond mane had been shaved down to a purple Mohawk (colored by Sharpie), she had numerous scratch and lighter-burn marks, and she'd lost a foot to an "experiment" with a box cutter. Ugly

Stepchild Barbie also had a torso with a black *V* shape drawn into her pelvic area, and outrageously large, red nipples on her boobs with fine black hairs drawn around the center (again, colored by that Matisse of Barbie abuse, le Sharpie). Tonight, Slick was at last ready to send Ugly Stepchild to her ignoble death.

Fletch laughed—it was an old joke that never got tired—but I was too panicked about what Slick was about to do.

"No! Don't!" I shouted.

But I was too late. Slick dramatically threw the Barbie onto the grill. The crowd cheered as poor Ugly Stepchild Barbie seared onto the metal.

I quickly ran back inside the restaurant, retrieved the fire extinguisher from beneath the cashier counter, and returned to the parking lot. I sprayed the grill, and the first-arrival crowd of about twenty people booed. I was supposed to be the party planner, not the party pooper.

"Guys!" I said. "No fires! THINK! We're in a drought. One stray spark could set this whole area on fire. Also, are you *trying* to bring Rancho Soldado High's fire marshal to this secret party?"

"Thrope," a few voices groaned.

I heard a few people mumble, "Sorry, Vic," as they snapped photos of the disgraceful corpse.

The remorseful people did not include Slick, who looked at me with such abject betrayal that my heart squirmed into a knot. Slick said, "What the fuck, Vic? It was just gonna be a quick, fun fire to launch the party. Damn. I've been planning that Barbie thing as a last-night-together surprise for us since forever."

Poor Ugly Stepchild Barbie, I thought. *I regret it had to end this way. You put in years of service and you deserved a better death than this, half melted and now suffocated by dry chemical fire extinguisher foam.*

To Slick, I said, "I'm sorry, sweetie. I wish you'd warned me." Slick knew I hated surprises I couldn't control. She should have known better than to think the words "quick" + "fun" + "fire" went together in any way that did not = "disaster." And did I really have to apologize to her *and* everyone here? About something so obvious, because drought, anyone?

If I wanted the opening of this party to recover, I guessed I did. "Sorry, everyone!" I added, in the same upbeat, positive tone I used when I petitioned the Town Council. No one looked that impressed, just like the Town Council. I knew there was really only one other word besides "sorry" I could invoke to save this situation. "Beer!" I called. "Out back. Go through the restaurant. Cash only."

A collective cheer marked a positive change of mood. "Pretty please help me, most beautiful and clever Barbie-murdering girl in the world?" I said to Slick, trying to swing her sulk away with blatant sucking up.

Slick jumped down from the back of the pickup truck. Reluctantly, she said, "Okay." I grabbed her and Fletch into the Cuddle Huddle. There'd been so much Cuddle Huddle during our last week together that my arms were sore. "I love you," I told them. "Thank you for finally throwing a Barbie onto a barbie. Tomorrow, I'll go light candles at church for Ugly Stepchild Barbie in your honor." My two BFFs were devout and weirdly sincere churchgoers, so offering to make amends in their place of worship always went a long way with them.

"Good plan," said Slick.

"Good cuddle," said Fletch.

"Good cuddle," I agreed.

We broke formation.

I walked over to the front entrance of the restaurant and, as we'd planned, Slick and Fletch joined me as door security to help with entry instructions. Jason "the Dunk" Dunker was the first in line to gain admittance inside. I asked him, "Who's your designated driver?" This party was going to be responsible about all the alcohol flowing so irresponsibly.

Without looking up from his phone, the Dunk said, "Olivier Farkas." As he was about to post a photo of Now-Dead Ugly Stepchild Barbie, Fletch snatched his phone just in time and played with the settings.

I said, "Jason. Phones need to be in data mode off for tonight. Take all the pictures you want tonight, but post tomorrow. I need your promise."

The Dunk shrugged. "What, is the fearsome Cuddle Huddle gonna make me sign a contract or something?"

"Just your word of honor," said Slick. "Or face forever shame in class history as the guy who broke the promise to turn off data on his phone for one freaking night, like that's so hard."

"'Kay," said the Dunk. "But there had better be enough beer to last the night."

"There is," I assured him.

"Where's the weed?" said Amy Beckerman, standing behind him.

The Dunk gestured to his backpack. "Fully stocked," he said.

"You may enter," I said, waving my hand to let the Dunk through.

It took hardly any time for the restaurant to fill up with partygoers. Within an hour, about two-thirds of the graduating class had shown up, and they quickly grooved into throes of beer-buying, beer-drinking, beer-ponging, and beer-dancing.

Fletch said, "Shift over! I need a drink. Any late arrivals are just going to have to be on the honor system with their phones."

"Agreed," said Slick, who had probably already sweated off five pounds in her skinny jeans from dancing to the beat of the music blasting from inside the restaurant. "This Zavala-Kim's shift is over." She grabbed Fletch with one hand, and me with her other, and dragged us inside Happies. Some old Spice Girls song was playing, and we immediately raced to the dance platform to get our middle school–age girl power dance on. We had to squeeze through a ton of people to get to the dance floor, as the music and beer were working their magic. And, so was Zeke.

The spry cherub inserted himself in the middle of our dance circle and started dance-waving his arms around like an octopus. I wasn't sure if he was trying to be funny or sexy, but the result was somewhere in between. Bizarre, yet endearing.

"*Tell me what ya want, what ya really, really want,*" he sang.

And Slick said, "I want for you to move out of the way, little brother!"

"Out of the way?" Zeke repeated, mock offended. "I'm the one who got all these people dancing to begin with."

"How's that?" Fletch asked.

"'Cuz I think the beer did it," I suggested.

Zeke said, "Think again, Team Cuddle Huddle. It was me dragging people up to the dance floor and wailing around them long enough to make them laugh and loosen up and have a good time!"

People were crowding around Zeke, imitating his octopus arm dance with great affection, so there may have been some accuracy to his boast.

Zeke did some break-dance moves around me, whirling across the floor with all the grace of a lumberjack, and then stood up and almost spat in my face he was so close. "Can I get you a beer?" he asked.

"Offer *all* of us, not *one* of us," said Slick, giving the side of her baby brother's shaved head a mild slap.

"Be useful, junior," said Fletch, shooing Zeke away. "Go forth and provide your elders with the beer they so richly deserve." She eyed Emerson Luong, Rancho's star track-and-field athlete bound for the University of Miami, and Raheem Anthony, its star computer programmer bound for Berkeley, drinking shots near the Make-Out Your Own Sundae Bar. She told us, "I foresee some dirty dancing in my future with those two." Zeke went for beer like a good junior as Fletch hightailed it toward the cute boys. Together, Fletch, Raheem, and Emerson were like a triumvirate of the smartest people at our school.

Slick asked me, "*DDR* match? Loser has to hear my industrious plans for this summer."

I laughed, because Slick always assumed I'd lose (she was usually right), and because Slick rarely had meaningful plans beyond scheduling her nap and all-important snack times.

I said, "I should make rounds and check on people first."

"Check on them how? People are drinking and dancing and making out. Exactly what they're supposed to be doing at a party. Situation looks under control to me. Maybe *I* have important news to share."

If Slick had breaking news she would have relayed it to me within seconds of it happening. I had more pressing issues to deal with. I said, "*DDR* soon. Promise. Right now I need to take a quick spin to monitor the ground troops."

She looked at me with the same disdain that had greeted me when I fire-extinguished Ugly Stepchild Barbie. "Are you having a party or masterminding a war battle, General Navarro?"

Bao Ling approached us, beer in hand. "Where's your bestie Thrope tonight?" I asked her.

Bao Ling said, "Thrope's not my bestie, but she can prove useful if you let her. Trust me. She paid me fifty bucks to translate for her this afternoon." She raised her beer in toast. "Beer money for tonight, thank you very much! And Thrope's going to a Ping-Pong tournament in Vegas tonight with her clients. She won't be bothering us."

"She has tentacles everywhere," I said, eyeing Bao Ling suspiciously.

"Not on me!" said Bao Ling.

Standing at Bao Ling's side, Slick tried to playfully bump her hips, but Bao Ling didn't seem to want to participate. "You don't dance?" Slick asked her.

"I dance!" Bao Ling said. "It just feels weird to dance with you two standing right here. I can see your third over there. Isn't she the one supposed to be dancing with you guys?"

We looked toward Fletch, now in a full-on Raheem Anthony/Emerson Luong dance sandwich by the Make-Out Your Own Sundae Bar.

"We dance with other people!" Slick proclaimed. "Come with me, let's *DDR* over there."

Bao Ling's face turned wide with awe. "Wow, am I being allowed inside the formidable BFF clique? I feel so special."

"We're not a clique!" Slick and I said in unison. Our response was automated and standard, since Slick, Fletch, and I had been forced to defend our BFFdom since first grade. We were inclusive. We hung out with other people. For real! We just liked each other's company the most.

"Jinx clique!" Bao Ling said.

"I gotta check on my guests," I told Slick. "Have fun without me." I looked toward Bao Ling. "You too, of course." I *didn't* mean Bao Ling, too, who still had a shadow of suspicion hanging over her in my opinion. But I was all about false sincerity in the name of trying to disprove the BFF clique accusation that had chased me, Slick, and Fletch through twelve years of the Rancho Soldado community pool and public school system.

Slick dragged Bao Ling away, calling back to me, "We'll be at the *DDR* having fun. Find us there if you want to do the same, loser!"

I walked to the long hallway leading outside, where the Dunk was set up for business, sitting at a folding table and chair, like a Girl Scout selling cookies.

"Brownie?" the Dunk asked me, holding out a tray of particularly yummy-looking chocolate goodness.

I rarely indulge in weed, mostly because I've seen how too much of it has made my brother basically comatose, but I said yes, mostly to be polite to the supplier. I needed to keep my wits about me to get through the night, but a brownie for later on, when the party wound down with me feeling up Jake, could be a nice treat.

The Dunk pulled the tray away from my hand as I was about to lift a brownie off it. "Two dollars," he said.

"What?" I said. "Don't tell me you've been charging people for brownies."

"Nothing good comes free."

"Sure it does. Emerson Luong brought the *free* Jell-O shots as a contribution to everyone's good times."

The Dunk sneered. "His mistake. Socialist. I prefer to exercise my right to free enterprise. Two dollars."

"You're at least supposed to comp the hostess, who made your business possible."

"Nah," said the Dunk, looking away, distracted by a group inside the restaurant. "Oooo, hookah me right in!" He stood up, tray in hand, and walked away, back toward the main assembly of party people. I followed him while pulling out two one-dollar bills from my pocket. I threw them onto his tray and lifted a brownie off it. "These better be good."

"I can't speak for the chocolate, but the weed oil is brought to you by Temecula's finest crop." He bowed down to me like an Asian businessman closing a transaction. "Pleasure doing business with you. A most fine party, General Navarro."

I wrapped my brownie in a napkin, put it in my purse for later, and watched the Dunk retreat to a corner where the stoners were situated. They were sharing a hookah pipe and exhaling their smoke onto a mountain of vanilla soft-serve, which was rapidly falling in the restaurant's hot air, mesmerizing the stoners with its melt. Someone handed the Dunk a cup of coffee, which he dunked a brownie into, as was his typical habit. I'm not sure if it's because his last name lent itself so well to the practice, or he just had a natural proclivity for soaked meals, but the Dunk's food never met a beverage it did not want to drown itself in. I blame Slick's tenth birthday party, when her mom demonstrated Oreos dipped in milk. It was like we saw a light go off in Jason's head—*ding!*—and he's been the Dunk ever since. That was the same party where some parents bestowed the nickname General Navarro on me, after I negotiated a peace settlement between Amy Beckerman and Bo Tucker, who'd gotten into a heated battle over the last seat during an epic battle of musical chairs. The adults couldn't get them to stop fighting, so I offered Bo my chair, which he wiped down with a sanitizing Wet Ones towelette from the packet he always had available in his pocket, and Amy whined, "That's not in the rules!" and I said, "The best rule is the one where you and Bo can both be winners," and she relaxed and it was a great party once again.

My eyes scanned across the restaurant, and I smiled, realizing how much the party had broken into the same social circles as in the school cafeterias we'd frequented since first grade. Our class, most of whom had known each other since elementary school, had graduated, but the high school archetypes they'd evolved into remained intact. Would it be the same at our reunions, five, ten, twenty years from now? The stoners had taken over one corner, while the jocks and cheerleaders congregated in the middle of the room. The smart people and nerds were in the back of the restaurant, while the art kids were making rounds, inspecting the yearbook and Happies wrappers decorations. The kids who crossed categories or didn't belong to any were the ones primarily occupying the dance floor.

I approached the hipster crowd who were lingering by the soft-serve ice cream machine. The air was too hot for too-cool threads, so the hipsters had abandoned their ironic T-shirts in favor of bare chests on the guys, and halter tops on the girls, with the exception of Amy Beckerman, who was wearing a tiny string bikini top and barely-there white denim shorts. She had been a chubster until middle school. The summer between eighth and ninth grades she went to fat camp and got really skinny, and she basically opted for next-to-naked apparel ever since.

"Everyone having a good time?" I asked the hipsters. They shrugged nonchalantly, which meant yes.

Amy Beckerman stepped up onto a stool, lifted the lid on the soft-serve machine, and then poured a bottle of vodka into it. "Is the fro-yo fat-free?" she asked.

"Yep," I said. "Full of chemicals, too."

"Awesome, now here's some more." She hiccupped and swayed a little as she placed the lid back onto the machine, and then she nearly fell off the stool. I held out my hand to help her back down onto the floor. "Thanks," she said, and hiccupped again.

It was too early in the party to have that major an exhale of booze breath. Concerned, I conscripted Olivier Farkas into service. "You'll look out for Amy?" I asked him.

"I guess," he said, eyeing Fletch and her dirty-dancing partners. "What's Genesis doing?" He had the tone of the sober. Not amused. Too alert. "Does she like Raheem or Emerson?"

"You know she's a free agent now," I reminded Olivier. "Don't hate."

Olivier—a bodybuilder who took out his aggression through lifting weights or eating power foods—chose to eat his stress about Fletch's new paramours. He reached into the bag of snacks on the counter, took out a dark green chip, and bit into it.

"Hey," I said, suspicious of the color of the chip. "Those chips weren't baked by the Dunk, were they?"

Olivier shook his head. "No way. You know I'm

straight edge. These are kale chips. I make them myself. Delicious, and an excellent source of fiber. Want one?"

"Sure," I said, mostly to be polite. Olivier extended the snack bag to me, and I reached in and then munched on a kale chip. "Mmmm," I said, faking delight but wanting to spit it out.

"Yes, yum!" said Amy Beckerman, who'd served herself her own customized culinary delight and was licking from the tip of her vodka-infused strawberry fro-yo.

"I need you to buddy system her tonight," I told Olivier.

"I already said I would. Give an order and trust it will be done, General Navarro," said Olivier, now eyeing Amy Beckerman's ass cheek spilling out of her shorts as she bent over for the fro-yo lick. "Don't micromanage."

He was right. I knew better. Did he? "No inappropriate moves on drunken girls," I said.

"I'm insulted," said Olivier.

"Don't be. I'm just doing my job."

"Don't worry." He sulked. "Genesis ruined me for all others."

I said, "I commend your excellent taste. Sorry, pal. Have fun, everybody!"

I moved next to the nerd assembly, gathered around the old pinball machine. "Hi, guys! Everyone having a good time?" They raised their beers to me, except for Bo

Tucker, who'd just finished his turn at the game and then had to rub sanitizer on his hands. "How soon till Thrope shuts the party down?" Bo asked, always the alarmist.

"She's not going to shut the party down," I said confidently. In my experience, I've learned that *sounding* confident is more important than *being* confident, because in the end, it doesn't matter if you're right or not. All that matters is that people think you are. I almost wanted to fast-forward to the end of the party, so I could right now have the satisfaction of seeing Thrope's face when she arrived for the real estate closing and found out what had happened tonight.

Bo said, "I heard she's had Mayor Jerry in some sort of sexual daze for years and that's how she got all her Town Council ordinances passed."

I sincerely believed that was possible, but I said, "Just because a woman is successful at her job doesn't mean she slept her way there." Was I secondhand high, or had I just defended Miss Ann Thrope in the name of feminism? I tried to high-five Bo in the spirit of camaraderie, but he did not raise his hand to greet mine. I knew better than to be offended; my gesture was pointless with a germophobe.

I next joined the protest radicals. The "rads," as they were called, were moshing to the Smiths song now playing as they congregated next to the rotating pie display case. "How's everyone doing over here?" I shouted over the music to Troy Ferguson, who was bound for the University of Oregon, and who would never, ever be someone whose sweet face I didn't look at and think, *You're the first guy I did it with.* I had no desire to have anything more than that one time with Troy, but there would always be a little bit of affection, and awkwardness.

"The rads are into it," said Troy, who understood—*really* understood—how I needed positive encouragement to get through experiences I was nervous about. "Hard to believe that when I come back from college next summer, this place will be gone."

I sighed. "We're getting out of Rancho just in time."

"Let's go into the theme park!" said Troy, swigging on a beer. "I want to see it before the land is razed."

"Absolutely not! And don't you dare try to lead a charge in that direction, okay? I promised Bev Happie."

Troy said, "Since when does General Navarro take commands? You're a leader, not a soldier."

I gave him an imploring look that said, *We shared a holy study hour together once on your lumpy twin bed with smelly boy* Star Wars *sheets, and if that sacred first time for both of us meant anything to you, you will not instigate the rads to storm the theme park.*

Troy smiled and patted my shoulder. "Don't worry, I won't try anything. But if *you* want to, I wouldn't say no."

I laughed. That was exactly the line Troy used to ignite the most memorable study session of my high school career.

The party was getting louder, drunker, wilder. Amy Beckerman stood on a stool by the soft-serve ice cream machine, holding yet another bottle of vodka over the top as the crowd around her chanted, "Pour! Pour! Pour!" Pieces of plaster were falling down from the ceiling from all the jumping around on the dance floor. The first wave of pukers were starting to line up at the bathrooms, and I heard someone yell, "Who's got a plunger?"

There were a million more fires to put out, but all I cared about was the one in my loins. I looked at a text that had just popped up on my phone, from Jake: `Get out here to the Chug Bug already. I need to throw you on top of all these stacks of dollar bills and have my dirty way with you.` "Laters, Troy," I said, and darted away, past the line of people at the bathrooms, through to the back parking lot, to my date with carnal destiny. The other fires could wait.

14

VIC NAVARRO,
ALE WENCH

10 p.m.

"General Navarro reporting for service," I announced to Jake as I stepped inside the Command Central that was the Chug Bug.

The line for beers was about twenty-five people deep, but Jake kept it moving swiftly, handing beers and taking money while talking to me. "Business is going *too* well. I'm going to be out of beer within the hour. Can you man the post here while I go down the road to Al's Wine 'n' Donuts to restock the supply? Shouldn't take me more than fifteen minutes, unless there's a line for lottery tickets."

I said, "There shouldn't be a line. Bev Happie gets *Death Valley Psychic News* text alerts when the Powerball jackpots get big, and she would have told me so I could play, too."

I looked at Jake's money box below the counter, stuffed high with twenties, tens, fives, and ones. Who needed the lottery with these earnings? Jake had plenty of cash now to resupply the beer to last through the night, and then some. He saw me eyeing the cash box, and then his foot lifted and latched around my ankle for a nice game of footsie. "Do you?" Jake asked.

"Do I what?"

Jake paused his beer transaction to look me squarely in the face, lift an eyebrow, and say, "Play." He handed a beer over to his customer, and then moved that cold hand to graze my warm behind.

"I play," I murmured.

"Great," said Jake. "Then play ale wench while I'm gone." He gave my rear a gentle slap with one hand, tipped his fedora at me with the other, and then placed his hat onto the counter so he could make both his hands into a heart shape on his chest. He leaned closer to whisper in my ear, "This was your best idea, ale wench. I'm forever grateful."

The heat was sweltering and I really owed Bev Happie an apology, because she and the *Death Valley Psychic News* were right. Oh yes, there would be some earthquakes happening here before the night ended. The hottest kind.

Jake returned his fedora to his head and pointed to a stack of index cards on the counter, next to an empty glass goldfish bowl with a few index cards placed inside. Jake said, "Encourage people to fill out the comment cards while I'm gone, would you? Gotta know what's working about the Chug Bug and what's not." He exited the beer truck, got into his mom's SUV, and took off.

I quickly typed a text to Lindsay before I resumed beer service to the next customer. Will you still love me even if I'm the dumbest dumbslut in San Francisco?

She responded immediately. I'll love you even more. But the competition for that title in this city is pretty fierce, so bring your best work ethic.

Aye, captain, I answered, determined to have my fun now. Thinking about where Jake and I would have our after-party made me acutely aware that in a week, I'd be living in a cramped group house of dirt-broke twenty-somethings, sleeping on an air mattress in my sister's bedroom, which would probably cool my sex drive. But a group house of lesbians was just what I needed, I told myself. Without the distraction of boys, I'd be able to focus on whatever I was supposed to focus on in the next stage of life. Like how I hadn't gotten into college and what the hell was I doing with my life and could this night never end so I didn't have to figure out these issues?

Raheem Anthony, next in line for beer, cleared his throat to get my attention. He asked, "Hello, Vic? Are you helping people or not?"

I put my phone down. "Sorry, buddy. How many?"

"Three."

"When do you leave for Berkeley?" I handed him the brews in exchange for a fistful of crumpled dollar bills.

"Not till September," said Raheem. "I've got some part-time programming work this summer in Las Vegas to keep me busy till then. Can't wait to get out of here."

"I'm going to be in San Fran. We'll practically be neighbors. We should hang out."

"Totally," said Raheem. He popped open one of the beers and lifted it in toast to me. "Great party. Thanks, Vic."

"Make sure Fletch isn't too hungover for her plane trip tomorrow," I said.

"Will do," said Raheem.

Leticia Johnson was next in line. "Two brewskis, please." I handed them to her. She paid me while inspecting the Chug Bug's exterior. "The design on the sides of the bus could use more flourish. Tell Jake I volunteer to graffiti paint it if I could photograph the work to use in my portfolio?"

I gave Leticia a comment card. "Write down your ideas and put the card in the fishbowl. I'll be sure to tell Jake to look for yours."

"Thanks."

"And Rhode Island School of Design made a *huge* mistake turning you down, Leticia. Next year, for sure!"

Leticia smiled.

I was surprised to see Jamila "Bashful" Beshara next in the beer line. "Two beers?" she asked shyly, not able to make eye contact with me, and not just because her head scarf was partially obscuring the top of her head.

"Are you sure, Bashful?" I asked, invoking her nickname so she could feel comfortable with me in this potentially awkward situation. I hesitated to hand over two bottles of cold brews to a devout Muslim, no matter how much her face, beaded in sweat from the heat and her scarf, appeared to need hydration.

Jamila nodded. "The beers are for my teammates. They're just about passed out over there." I looked past the beer line and saw a couple of girl jocks slumped against the fence, their heads on each other's shoulders.

"Save your money," I told Jamila. "If they're too passed out to come get their own beers, they're not okay to drink more. I have all the restaurant's leftover water bottles lined up against the wall over there. Take some. They're free. Hydration encouraged."

"The girls will be bummed if I return without beers," said Jamila. "I don't like to let my teammates down."

"I know, so tell them I said no. This is not on you. They can come back for more beers when they're able to stand on their own two feet."

"Okay," said Jamila, looking relieved.

"Hey, I heard you got a soccer scholarship to USC. That's amazing. Congrats!"

I had played junior varsity with Jamila during our freshman and sophomore years. I was a decent enough player, but Bashful Beshara was a true star. This past year, she became varsity captain and led the team to state semifinals, no small feat since the rest of the squad members were good athletes but also party girls. I had been too busy with ATEC to go out for soccer senior year, but I always tried to go to games just for the awe of watching Jamila play. Though painfully shy on a normal day, like many great performers, she completely came alive on a stage—or a soccer field, in her case. She played in fierce and graceful leaps and bounds, like a world-class dancer, and not even her perpetual head scarf could get in her way when she eyed a goal opportunity.

Jamila's mouth moved into a very sweet, shy grin. "Thanks. So what're you doing next year, Vic?"

Not going to USC, I thought. My mood threatened to take a negative shift as I realized what I felt toward Jamila, whom I genuinely liked: major jealousy. I was never going to get a soccer scholarship, but I would have liked to have gotten into USC. Why had I been such a dumbfuck who didn't apply to any other college? While I've learned how important it is to go through life *sounding* confident even if you're not, what I now realized was that maybe the appearance of confidence had inadvertently made me overconfident. Certainly it had where college applications were concerned.

Someone toward the back of the line shouted out, "The line's moving too slowly! Hey, General Navarro, are you campaigning for office or operating a beer truck?"

Zeke stepped into the Chug Bug, once again appearing out of nowhere. "Need some help?" he asked.

"I guess I do," I said. "The crowd is getting angsty."

"Know what your problem is?" Zeke asked.

"I'm talking too long to the customers?" I turned around to say good-bye to Bashful, but she was already gone, and the next person in line was Bo Tucker, sighing in irritation and flashing the ticking stopwatch on his phone, to let me know I was taking too long.

Zeke said, "Yeah. And not drinking enough." He popped open a beer and then pulled out a wedge of lime from his pants pocket and inserted it into the top of the beer bottle. He handed it to me like it was a precious gift.

I said, "I don't want a lime that's been in your sweaty pocket all night."

He took the lime from the beer bottle and tossed it outside onto the ground. "So don't have the lime. I went to get you a beer a while ago and cut the lime for you then. Never found you, so I drank your beer but held on to the lime in case you'd want it later in another one."

"Thank you?" I said, meaning it skeptically.

"You're welcome!" Zeke said cheerfully. "Remember: With great beer power comes great responsibility. You've thrown together an awesome party, but we gotta keep the line moving, ale wench." He snapped his fingers, like *chop-chop*.

When Jake called me "ale wench," the words sounded like the hottest enticement. From Zeke, they sounded absurdly funny. I giggled and took a swig of beer. Yes, that was exactly the refreshment I needed. The beer *and* Zeke. Whoever nabbed this sweet, oversize stud for a boyfriend would be one helluva lucky guy.

Jake returned about a half hour later. "Powerball jackpot's up to almost two million. Not a mega-lottery, but somebody ought to tell Bev Happie." He handed me a lotto ticket. "Here, I bought you one to give to her, as a little thank-you for tonight." He looked at his XL-sized baby brother. "Make yourself useful, little man. Al's was out of ice because we pretty much cleared them out earlier. Go check the freezer room and see if there's any more supply in there."

"I'll come with," I said with some reluctance—because I really wanted to be on ale wench duty by Jake's side. But I needed to monitor the inside situation again. The noise from the restaurant had been getting louder, more boisterous, and I'd heard glass breaking and reports of dancing on countertops (which wasn't forbidden—I just wanted to see it in action).

As Zeke and I passed through the throngs, he asked, "So when can my band play?"

"You're still serious about that? Where's your bandmates?"

"They can be here within half an hour once I alert them."

"How can you be so sure they're still up?"

"They're musicians, dude. The night's just starting for our kind."

We stopped at the freezer room so I could unlock it for him before I proceeded back to check on the party in the rest of the space. But I was stopped from opening it by the lob of a marshmallow to the side of my head.

"What the fuck?" I said.

"Please don't curse," said the shooter. "It's so unlady-like." I turned my head to see Evergrace Everdell. She was holding a marshmallow gun and wearing (unironically) a Robin Hood hat on her head, like she'd come to save this party.

"Or you'll do what?" I said. "Lob another fucking marshmallow at me?"

To prevent just a scenario, I tried to grab the weapon from Evergrace's hand, but she resisted, and so began a ridiculous waste of time on a tug-of-war over a marsh-mallow gun. Evergrace said, "You'd better let go, or I'll alert Thrope." She paused. "Or maybe I already have."

I let go.

15

RAGE AND THE ICE
SCREAM MACHINE

10:30 p.m.

"DID YOU TELL THROPE?" I demanded of Evergrace Everdell.

"I don't know," she said. "Did you or did you not invite me here tonight?"

I knew I should have invited Evergrace, but she had too much history as a tattletale to school administration figures. Her complaint file was notorious. No one told her about the junior class trip to Six Flags. She didn't get invited to the homecoming game pep rallies. Team LARP never sent her the alert for *Star Wars* cosplay day.

I didn't invite her because I didn't want to risk her telling Thrope. But I tried to save face by telling her, "I guess we forgot. Technically, you're not on our class phone tree because you were homeschooled, and that's how we sent out the invites. So sorry about that!"

Not sorry. Happies was indeed for everyone, but could be better enjoyed without guests having to worry about inadvertently offending the fragile sensibility of Evergrace Everdell. She brushed off my insincere apology and focused her eyes on Zeke and, with all the casualness of a random encounter at the grocery store checkout line, said to him, "I heard you're running for president of the Gay-Straight Alliance next year?"

Zeke shrugged. "I don't know. Maybe."

"You should!" said Evergrace. "Too bad I'm no longer eligible for a second term 'cuz I'd totally do it all over again. But I could coach you to run for office if you want."

"Pretty sure I'd run unopposed," said Zeke. "No one even ran for posts in the GSA till you wanted to be president. No one actually cares who's president, I think? Isn't it just something to put on college applications?"

Evergrace said, "It's so much more than that! There are many important responsibilities like—"

"Excuse me!" I interrupted.

"What?" both Evergrace and Zeke said.

I said, "Did you tell Thrope about the party or not?" Bao Ling had said Thrope was in Vegas for the night, but that was less than an hour's drive away. She could be gunning her way here right now for all I knew. Where had I put that brownie I procured from the Dunk? Now would be a good time to take a bite into mellow because fear was not an option.

I couldn't hear Evergrace's response over the roar of the crowd in the main part of the restaurant, chanting "AMY! AMY! AMY!" Then there was a collective scream, followed by the sound of glass bottles being thrown onto the floor and shattering. Concerned, I followed the sound of the commotion, and found Amy Beckerman standing on top of the long countertop for single diners. She was country line dancing to the song "Party in the U.S.A." along with Nestor Castillo, the most danciest, losingest quarterback in the history of Rancho Soldado High School. Amy's side of the dance, though, was more a striptease, and every time she reached the end of the countertop that was opposite the ice cream machine, she played with the unstrung loose ends of her string bikini top and shimmied toward it, as if she was going to take it off and throw it into the opened pour top. And each time she seemed like she would throw it in, the crowd shouted "AMY! AMY! AMY!" and when she didn't, the people assembled around her on the floor smashed their finished beer bottles onto the ground.

Zeke said, "She really knows how to put the *tease* in *striptease.*"

"Do I need to stop this?" I asked him. If Thrope was on her way, I needed a contingency plan, but there was too much noise and chaos for me to focus on anything but what was going on directly in front of me.

All around, classmates who weren't dancing had their phones on Amy and Nestor's dance, recording her every move. Zeke said, "I'm thinking, yeah."

"How?" Getting a drunk girl down from her pedestal when revelers were cheering her on was an impossible and thankless task. And where the fuck was Olivier Farkas, who was supposed to be monitoring Amy and had been insulted when I made him promise—twice—to buddy system her?

Zeke answered by jumping up onto the counter and joining in the line dancing. He tried to bump and grind Nestor Castillo, who was not having that from another dude, and immediately jumped down onto the ground. That took care of half the problem immediately. Then Zeke started performing a *Magic Mike* knockoff routine that looked ridiculous, but also hilarious. The crowd chanted, "Zeke! Zeke! Zeke!" and Amy actually looked relieved to have the attention taken away from her, like she'd been trapped by her own exploits and had needed the Zeke diversion to escape. She looked at me plaintively, and I moved closer to give her a hand to step down.

"Dizzy!" Amy said. I put my arm around her to hold

her up, and spied Olivier Farkas watching us from the side of the room. I dragged Amy to Olivier, and she plopped down onto the floor for a break, or a nap, I'm not sure which.

"You promised, Olivier," I said. "Don't let me down."

"Sorry, Vic," Olivier said. "I got distracted by that over there." He pointed toward the Make-Out Your Own Sundae Bar, where Fletch was dipping a spoon into a bowl of ice cream. Fletch took a lick, and then turned to kiss Emerson Luong. Fletch pulled back, took another lick of ice cream, and turned to her other side to kiss Raheem Anthony. Damn, I had no idea my girl had that level of party trick in her. Applause.

"Don't look," I advised Olivier. "It'll all be over by morning, and she'll be gone for the next year, at least."

Olivier looked like he might weep. Amy placed his head on her shoulder, and then placed her own head against his.

Perfect. Those two were settled. Now I just needed to control the beer bottle smashing. Or did I?

Once again, I was shot in the face with a marshmallow. "Guess what, Miss I-Only-Invite-Classmates-on-the-Official-Class-Phone-Tree?" Evergrace Everdell taunted me.

"WHAT?" I yelled. I had more important demands on my time than handling Evergrace Everdell's brand of nonsense.

Evergrace said, "You're worried about Thrope showing up? What you really should be worried about is the two busloads of Happies parked outside."

There were not enough variations of the word "fuck" to express the panic I felt. A convergence of bona fide Happies at the Last Call at Happies party was one possibility I hadn't factored into my In Case of Disaster planning.

The party couldn't survive an intrusion of this proportion.

Bam! Bam! Bam! Evergrace answered my pause of incredulity at this bad news by popping a barrage of three more marshmallows at my head.

"Could you not do that?" I screeched, as she reloaded her gun from the marshmallow ammunition belt around her waist. "And who told the Happies about the party?" I was thinking aloud, not really expecting an answer to that question, but Evergrace had one.

Evergrace said, "I posted about the party on the Happies online message board. I didn't alert Thrope but I did alert the Happies. I thought at least *I* should be inclusive about the party since you so rudely weren't, and the Happies are the people who'd most want to enjoy the restaurant one last time."

"Tattletale," I muttered. Just as I'd anticipated.

Everbitch didn't hear me, and continued on. "But I just

saw some of them pulling bolt cutters out from the coach storage area. I think the Happies came to tear down the fence to the old theme park before it's too late."

I had to nip this problem in the bud immediately. I looked toward Zeke, still dancing on the countertop, smiling at me like all hell wasn't breaking loose.

"HELP ME!" I shouted.

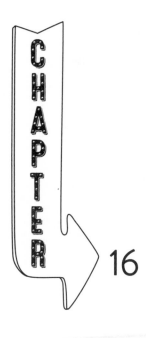

16   EARTHQUAKE WEATHER: ACTUALLY POSSIBLE

11 p.m.

Before going outside, I first took a quick peek through my cardboard window peephole. I saw two tour buses parked in the outside lot, hordes of Happies spewing from their depths. The fan folk were mostly middle-aged, wearing vintage Happies theme park uniforms, old Happies soda jerk hats, and Happies sashes lined with pins and patches, just like the man who had approached Bev at graduation. They kept busy pulling items out of the storage area below the bus: a ladder, large floodlights, what looked to be a mobile cotton candy machine, and many tubs of beer. The bolt cutters were a waste, though, because the Happies theme park fence was cement, not wire.

Zeke stood next to me at the window, his multi-colored pompadour brushing my cheek. He leaned in to my ear and sang aloud from the tune playing on the restaurant speakers. *"You gotta FIGHT . . . for your RIGHT . . . to PAAAAARty. . . ."*

"This is a disaster," I muttered.

"Nah," he said, unconvincingly.

"I don't know what the hell to do," I confessed. My veneer of false confidence had disappeared. I didn't even have that to count on in this situation.

Zeke grabbed my hand and I felt oddly comforted by the big warmness of it. "So we'll do it together."

He led me outside, and somehow, I found my courage.

I approached a plump, late-middle-aged woman wearing a vintage candy-striped Happies waitress uniform, with a sash full of medals and ribbons. She was holding a megaphone, so I guessed she was in charge of this brigade, which I feared could grow exponentially bigger. Bev Happie always said anytime she saw a Happies fan decked out in memorabilia, she knew at least two dozen more were following. They swarmed like ants.

I cleared my throat and said, "Can I help you? I assume you know Happies is closed now. No longer in business."

"HAPPIES IS CLOSED?" the lady yelled into her megaphone, only she addressed the tour bus people, not me.

"HELL, NO!" the crowd responded, like they'd been practicing on the bus.

I said, "No, really, it's closed! I'm so sorry! Bev Happie would be honored you came to the restaurant tonight, but . . ."

The megaphone lady said, "We're not here for the restaurant, darling. We got in all the burgers and fries we wanted before we left Vegas."

She left me no other option than the scariest tactic available to me: outright honesty. "I'm Victoria Navarro, and I'm in charge here tonight. I'm afraid I have to ask you to leave—"

"I'm Joan, sweethearts," the megaphone lady interrupted. "And we've come too far and just spent too much money on supplies at Home Depot for us to return to Vegas now!"

"Vegas isn't that far," said Zeke, taking her literally.

She said, "We don't live in Vegas, cutie hair patootie. We're Happies who get together a few times a year *in* Vegas. We're from all over. Imagine our delight when we saw the message posting about the Happies' final party here tonight." *I'm going to kill you, Evergrace Everdell.* "No chance we wouldn't take this grand opportunity for one last visit!"

Joan turned to address drivers of the tour buses through her megaphone. "TURN THOSE HEADLIGHTS ON! WE NEED SOME LIGHT ON THE FENCE!"

"No headlights!" I ordered, to no effect whatsoever. The bus headlights turned on, illuminating the fence quite effectively. "Don't do this!" I begged Joan.

Zeke pulled a ten-dollar bill from his pocket and flipped it in her direction. "Maybe this would help to get those buses turned back around?"

Joan let out a giant laugh. "Aren't you adorable," she said to Zeke.

Zeke said, "I'm very dangerous, actually. And I'll need to defend Happies against this intrusion."

Joan said, "If you're dangerous, I'm the ghost of Mary Happie. And thousands of dollars couldn't keep us away."

"Millions?" Zeke offered.

Joan laughed again. But I knew: If Zeke had millions (or even thousands), he'd have given it to them without hesitation to save my ass.

And then, a huge rumble from down the highway alerted me that the busloads of Happies weren't my night's biggest problem. The situation was so much worse. A biker gang, fifty or so riders in all, on very loud Harleys, rode into the parking lot.

"Now *this* is melt-your-dick-off awesome," said Zeke. I looked at him like, *Not helping!* "Also terrifying," Zeke added.

It all happened so fast. A gust of dirt like a whirling dervish swept across the parking lot, and the bikers stopped their Harleys in a formation, five aisles of ten or so bikers, behind one leader who stopped his bike front and center. The guys wore leather jackets and chaps, with bandannas on their ponytailed heads, and they were old-school patriarchy, with their female companions sitting behind them dressed the same, but with more boob action rising up from beneath their half-zippered jackets.

They were zombie-level scary-looking, and somehow it was up to me to protect my classmates from them.

This was not how I'd foreseen the night going. The worst thing that had ever happened in the history of a Happies senior class party was my dumbfuck brother and his friends and their ditch-digging mission. That now seemed quaint in comparison. Nowhere in my memory databank of Happies' parties was there a potential gang war between competing caravans of biker dudes and elderly Happies disciples. Neither faction of whom had been invited.

As the engine noise quieted down, my classmates began to stream outside to see what the commotion was about. There was a palpable excitement in the air. I could feel it in my sweaty armpits and panicked breath. I looked to the side of the restaurant, hoping Jake would appear to help or take control of the situation, as the eldest local dude representing Rancho Soldado High School's alumni tonight, but he was nowhere to be seen. Nor were Fletch and Slick. The wall of defense was just me and an overgrown man-boy with rainbow-poufed middle hair and tunnel ears.

The motorcycle leader stepped off his bike. He looked like Hulk Hogan, with leathered skin to go along with his leather jacket, a long goatee growing from his chin, and . . . now that I could see closer, Happies badges and pins bedazzling his jacket, along with the Happies' patches sewn onto leather sides?

"Joan!" he called to the megaphone lady.

"DELROY!" she megaphoned. "YOU OWE ME TWENTY BUCKS! TOLD YA WE'D GET HERE FIRST."

Delroy the biker said, "You got a head start. Traffic cops don't like making way for the Happies' Angels down the Strip." He looked around. "Anyone in charge here?"

Zeke boldly stepped forward. "I am." I was startled, but impressed. When had that boy grown a pair? Certainly his dick had *not* melted off in this heat.

"I got this," I murmured to him. Maybe it was adrenaline, but my false confidence had kicked back in.

"You're sure?" he whispered.

"I guess," I whispered. Zeke was by my side, backing me up. I could handle this.

"Actually, I'm in charge," I announced, and approached the bike leader. "I'm Victoria Navarro. Bev Happie authorized me to throw a *private* event here tonight. I'm so sorry if the word didn't get out that Happies is no longer open to the public."

"Aren't you a misinformed sassy lassie," Delroy said cheerfully. He walked toward me with his hand outstretched, and grabbed mine into a death grip handshake. "Nice to meet you, Victoria Navarro. I'm Delroy Cowpoke. Pleased as could be to be called forth to celebrate this heavenly occasion."

I was too scared to actually laugh at his name, or laugh that he said it with exactly no irony, but I did hear Zeke snort. "What occasion is that?" I asked.

"Why, we're going to bring the Happies theme park back to life for one last party before Bev sells off the land. Of course, darlin'!"

"You can't do that!" I beseeched Delroy Cowpoke. "I promised Bev no one would go into the theme park."

"And I'm sure you meant it when you promised it," he answered.

"You know there are ghosts of dead Union Army soldiers in the cemetery, right? And the ravine is spooked by the spirits of Native American warriors! They don't like intruders!" I couldn't believe I'd tried Bev Happie's old line, but what other defense did I have against two busloads *and* a biker gang of Happies?

Delroy Cowpoke laughed. "We're counting on that!"

I tried to stop this madness with all I had left—pretty much, nothing. "The fence is locked! Only Bev has the key to open it!"

Delroy said, "No problem." He picked up a piece of dirt from the ground and crumbled it through his fingers. "See how dry this land is? All it needs is one good earthquake to shake it loose." He turned around to address his troops. "Happies' Angels Troop 119, please rev your engines." A deafening roar zoomed across the parking lot as the bikers revved their engines. "Full throttle!" Delroy instructed, like he was the captain of the fucking starship *Enterprise*. The bikers throttled their engines, creating a huge sound wave. The Happies bus people, and Zeke and I, and some of my partying classmates who'd wandered outside, all placed our hands over our ears and ducked for cover in case window glass went flying. It was a good thing I'd lined the front windows of the restaurant with cardboard, or those windows would have blown out immediately from their proximity to the throttle. "Harder!" Delroy commanded. The bikers revved harder, and louder, and I swear I thought I was going to lose my hearing entirely.

POP! POP! POP! A window on the bus closest to the biker gang shattered. There was no opportunity for the crowd to react, though, because in the next instant, the theme park fence built into the dry, parched earth fell over. Just like that.

Cheers erupted from the Happies bus people, and my classmates. My heart a little bit died.

The portal to the other world had been successfully broken by the seismic noise. The busloads of Happies ignored their shattered bus windows and immediately swarmed over to the giant clown face entrance, stepped over the fence on the ground, and streamed into the theme park, with the partying senior class of Rancho Soldado High School following behind them.

"Fuck!" was all I could say. I could handle some goofball drunk classmates dancing on countertops and damaging restaurant fixtures and backing up toilets. I could have handled Thrope trying to shut down the party. But this? This level of chaos was not one I could even begin to control.

This craziness was all Bev Happie's fault. Leaving a teenager in charge of a major party was a huge mistake. Totally irresponsible.

"Yippee!" Delroy Cowpoke shouted. "Let's go!" The

bikers stepped off their bikes. Delroy looked at me and said, "Don't worry, I'll tell Bev I did it. Me and her got a history. I always promised her that one day I'd show her real earthquake weather. Harley-style! Yee-HAH!"

He led the bikers into the theme park as, once again, I stood in place, dumbfounded and unable to move. I didn't even speak up to charge them admission.

Zeke snapped his fingers in my face, trying to break me out of my shock. "I hear Clown Town's now open for business. Shall we?" He extended his arm to me like a gentleman.

I told Zeke, "I guess if I can't beat 'em, might as well join 'em."

I was crushed by my failure to anticipate this madness. But admittedly, my heart was also a little bit reborn at the prospect of experiencing the theme park before it was gone.

I borrowed Zeke's arm until I could find and take Jake's instead, and together we ventured forth toward the forbidden land.

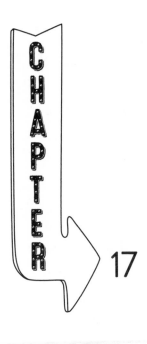

17

FEENIN' THE FIRES
11:30 p.m.

"**B**RIGHTNESS BEACONS!" Joan wailed into her megaphone. A small army of Happies surrounded her, carrying lawn chairs, musical instruments, food and ice chests, and lighting. Through her booming mouthpiece, Joan directed the Happies carrying floodlights. "You, take that one to the Ghost Cemetery. You guys, take the smaller lights and line them up in Bygone Rancho. You, with the flashing lights. Take them to Lovers Lane."

The Happies needed no maps or further directions. They immediately splintered and headed off to their disparate locations, which apparently they remembered even though the park had been closed for fifteen years. They had cheat sheets, too, as a few of them wore vintage Happies T-shirts with the old park's map printed on the backs.

I embrace you, Chaos.

What else was I supposed to do? Call Bev Happie and be like, *Er . . . sorry, Bev, but two bus caravans of Happies and a Happies-obsessed troop of Hells Angels sort of . . . um . . . created an earthquake to topple the theme park fence. Now everyone's trespassed into the park and it's no longer a senior class party happening in your restaurant, but, like, a middle-of-the-night, macabre desert carnival. Oops? All the drunk-ass minors are the least of my complications tonight! Ha-ha, it's funny, right? Are you still there, Bev?*

I was too scared to call Bev or some other Responsible Adult Person in Charge for help, and I had no idea where Fletch and Slick were, so I consulted my usual default, and sent a text to Lindsay.

So a biker gang literally just broke down the fence to the theme park and the party has moved in there. It's sort of amazing, but also terrifying. What the fuck should I do?

Lindsay texted back: Holy shit! Are you safe?

I clarified: It's a Happies biker gang.

She replied with ☺ ☺ and this wisdom: Fuck it. Enjoy it. Find out if Pinata Village is still there. It was kiddie rides surrounded by trees with piñatas hanging down from most every branch. It was mental. Send me pix!

Before we followed the crowd's surge past the tumbled fence and into the old Clown Town, I first stopped at the Chug Bug. But the beer truck's lights were off, the raised roof down, the counters folded in. The Chug Bug was closed for business, apparently, and Jake was nowhere to be found.

"Where do you think your brother went?" I asked Zeke.

"Follow the skirt trail. At least that's what Mom says when she can't find him." Zeke pointed toward a pack of tipsy girls wobbling around another giant clown face— smaller than the one at the entrance, but big enough to slide all over. I didn't address Zeke's put-down of Jake because another form of disrespect commanded my attention, and I was immediately called to action when one of the girls lit a sparkler and tried to insert said sparkler up the clown's nose. I raced toward the group loitering on the innocent, fallen clown. It was bad enough a Barbie had been senselessly tortured tonight. I wouldn't let it happen to the clown, too. Not on my watch. I pulled out the sparkler from the clown's nostril, threw it to the side, and furiously stepped on it to put out the flames. "Guys! Please, nothing flammable in here!"

My classmates laughed, insincerely mumbled "Sorry, Vic," and moseyed on down Main Street, not a fire care in the world. "Any more sparklers in your possession?" I called to them.

Leticia Johnson turned back my way and handed me a plastic container filled with sparklers. "Here, General Navarro."

"Thank you. Have fun I guess, but use common sense when it comes to fire safety!"

"Okay, Grandma," said Leticia, and returned to her group of wobbling friends.

"I give up," I said to Zeke. "I need a breather from trying to be the boss." I was *inside* Happies theme park. Living the dream! I lay down on top of the giant clown face, and Zeke joined me. We stared up at the night sky burning bright and clear with stars. The air smelled like beer and desert wildflowers and excitement as, in the distance, the Happies sang the Happies song, and my classmates joined in. All around were the sounds of people laughing and celebrating. I was terrified, and waiting for the next disaster—but also proud. Inadvertently, I had made this joy possible. If I could just keep the land from going up in flames that would spread across the desert, my own joy would be complete.

"Is it disrespectful that my fat ass is nestled deep down into the clown's eyelid?" Zeke asked me.

"Your sweet ass is probably the most gentle love that poor clown's had in years."

"You really know how to dirty talk a dude."

"Thank you."

Zeke was not the dude I wanted to be dirty talking, but he was a surprisingly fun substitute.

I asked Zeke, "Do you ever worry about the tunnels in your ears getting caught on something? Like, you walk by a tall cactus plant and a branch hooks in and pulls your earlobe out?"

Pause. "Now I do."

I stood up and extended my hand to Zeke. "Just lookin' out for you, little bro. Next time you think you want to pierce some part of your anatomy, please consult me first."

Zeke jumped to his feet, practically bumping me with his groin he was so close. "Which part of my anatomy?"

I rolled my eyes. "*Every* part."

We started walking down Main Street, and our steps fell in sync with each other's. Neither the bright stars nor the full moon offered enough light to guide our way, and there was no operational lighting in the park. While the lampposts were still standing, their power sources had been extinguished years ago, the lanterns cracked or broken, with many of the posts covered in graffiti. The

Happies had set up intermittent floodlights on the ground, but those only provided so much help with seeing in the dark, so people were using their phones for light, or the flashlights that the Happies bus and biker crews had brought inside with them.

"All these dumbfucks are posting pictures online," I said, looking at all the lit phones brightening the dark space like disco-ball glitter light bursts. "I can just feel it."

Zeke said, "They've been posting pictures all night. You really can't be so naive as to think your honor system for staying off social media actually worked?" I stared him down, and Zeke laughed. "Dear, sweet Vic. I'm pretty sure I saw people in the restaurant looking at a page devoted to Amy Beckerman's stripper dancing *while it was happening*. You know that most everyone who turned the data mode off their phone to get past you into the restaurant turned that feature back on as soon as they were in line for beer, don't you?"

I sighed. I knew. "Way to deny my denial."

"That would make a great band name. Deny My Denial."

"Or a great name for a Happies mega-dessert. A calorie explosion, like caramel-covered vanilla ice cream on top of a piece of coconut cake, with a piece of RASmatazz pie sandwiched inside the cake layers."

"WANT!" Zeke held his phone from his face and took a selfie while licking his lips. "So I'll remember the idea," he said.

"You were looking at people's phones during Amy Beckerman's dance routine to see if they were posting pictures of *you*, weren't you?"

"No," Zeke said weakly. "What I'm saying is: The word is out. Either the cops come, or Thrope comes, or both. It's gonna happen, so why not just enjoy yourself in the moment?"

The moment! It should have been shared with Fletch and Slick. If I was going to explore the park on its last night in existence, my companions were supposed to be my soul sisters. Where were they, anyway? I took my phone from my pocket to see a ton of messages I'd missed from Fletch and Slick, asking me the same thing: *Where ARE you?*

"Give me that," said Zeke. He grabbed it from my hand and slipped it into his back pocket. "There's a fucking miracle happening here right now. Live it! Don't text it."

Damn, now that he was a junior, he thought he could be Mr. Bossy? As someone who was also very bossy, I liked it—to a point. I heard the *ding* of a new text message coming into my phone, and instinctively I lunged for his pocket, but Zeke pulled the phone out before I could grab it. He held his arm up so I couldn't reach it. Zeus have mercy, how tall was he now? I used to be able to grab a remote control or video console from him with no problem. I was forced to jump high in an attempt to grab my phone, but Zeke retaliated by tossing it as hard and as far as he could.

"I can't believe you just did that!" I screeched.

"You can find it in the morning," Zeke said, nonchalant, like he'd just given me a paper cut and not detached a vital part of my anatomy. My most crucial link to the Cuddle Huddle had been dismantled; now how was I going to find them? And I couldn't remember a significant event that had happened without live-texting with my sister about it. Nonsignificant events, too. Hell, *any* events.

"No, *you* go find it! NOW!" I shrieked at Zeke.

"No," said Zeke, unconcerned. He took a bandanna out of his other pocket and tied it around a tree branch a few feet away. "Here. Now we know where the phone was tossed from. We'll look over there once it's light again."

Where he'd thrown the phone appeared, from what little light we had, to be a field of weeds taller than me, probably slithering with snakes. "That was my personal property! What if I actually do need to call the cops, if this party gets more out of hand?"

"Won't need to," Zeke said. "Have a little faith. There's a method to my madness."

"What method is that?"

Zeke opened his chubby arms wide, and gestured around the park. "Here! Now! Be present! You're fucking welcome!"

That was when we heard the firecrackers.

"We can use my phone if there's an emergency," Zeke said between wheezes, as together we ran through Bygone Rancho, past the fake Western-town-building facades, with signs for the Wanderlust Hotel and the Bawdy Saloon, hung a right toward the noise, and found ourselves with a group of Happies bikers setting off firecrackers. This wasn't how I'd hoped to discover Pinata Village, watching as motorcycle dudes, seated on toppled-over kiddie airplanes and trains and dolphins, dabbled in dangerous, noisy fire hazards. They didn't seem at all concerned by the nearby overgrown trees, which were littered with tons of sun-faded pieces of papier-mâché and cardboard—relics of former piñatas.

"There's Mega-Joan. Ask her for help," said Zeke.

A Responsible Adult Person in Charge! Well, sort of. We ran to her and I begged, "Please, Joan, tell them to have their fun, but not with fire! The land is so dry here and . . ."

Before I could finish, Joan held up her megaphone and announced, "No firecrackers, please. NO FIRE-MAKING AT ALL, IN FACT!" I'm not too proud to admit it was a huge relief to have a way-more-intimidating-than-me-person putting the bikers on notice, loudly, about how to appropriately celebrate. The bikers immediately ceased setting off firecrackers and returned the unused supplies to the storage trunks on their motorcycles.

Classic Mom deferral. Thanks, Mega-Joan.

I could try to put out fires on the ground, but the fires in the loins? The horny bastards of Rancho Soldado High School were certainly igniting them.

Fine. Whatever. Enjoy yourselves. That'd be me and Jake later tonight, once I located him.

"There's a *lot* of booty-grinding happening in this park tonight," Zeke observed as we strolled into the old Lovers Lane miniature golf course, where we saw couples, some triples, even a quartet, in full throes of making out, feeling up, *truly* enjoying themselves.

"So what *is* feenin'?" I asked Zeke, remembering the song Slick had told me he put on the sexy mix they delivered to Thrope's neighbors earlier in the day.

Zeke dropped to his knees, clutched his hands to his heart, and serenaded me in '90s boy-band style. *"All the chronic in the world couldn't even mess with you / You are the ultimate high / You know what I'm saying baby?"*

"I don't," I said. "That's why I asked." His singing voice was surprisingly good: strong, confident, and dare I say it, super sexy. I'd never heard him sing before without the loud, plugged-in musical accompaniment of his basement bandmates. "If you were into girls, I might consider jumping your bones immediately."

Zeke wrapped his arms around the backs of my legs, pressing the side of his face into my knees. Then he pulled back, stretched his arms toward the sky and pressed his hands against his heart as he serenaded me with, *"I can't leave you alone / You got me feenin'."*

"So it's stalker-speak for love craving?"

"Basically. From, like, a really sucky stalker who smokes too much weed."

I laughed. "Get up before some feenin' really happens, please." Zeke resisted standing up, so I lightly kicked his pompadour pouf, and he stood up. I asked him, "Hey, you know what really sucks?"

"Intermission. That's what sucks."

"What?" I asked, laughing harder, forgetting about the rant I'd been about to spew.

"Intermission," Zeke repeated. "Just finish the fucking show!"

I'd been about to bring up an important topic, and he was concerned about intermission? "Explain yourself."

Zeke said, "Unless a performance is, like, four hours long, there's really no need to break up the energy. I won't see a show if I know there's an intermission. Swear to God, won't even buy a ticket."

"You think you're so punk. You think every song should be two minutes, and you can kill a show in just an hour's performance and leave the audience hungering for more before you walk off stage in a very loud blaze of sweaty glory. Am I right?"

"You're exactly right. Imagine if you'd been at a Ramones show at CBGB during its heyday. You wouldn't want a break from that madness!"

"Yeah, but that's a bad example. Like, if I'm watching *Titanic* with my girls, again, that's what? Four hours? We need a break halfway through!"

"Because you need some chips 'n' guac and Doritos pizzas to help alleviate that sinking feeling you're getting?"

"Very punny." I shoved him. "Hey, speaking of shows, where are your bandmates? Shouldn't they be here if you're going to perform?"

"They're musicians. They never show up earlier than taco'clock. So they should be here any second. Too bad there's no real food besides pie, if there's even any of that left."

"Ugh, don't remind me how hungry I am."

"The Happies should've brought a taco truck with them! That's what really sucks."

Now I remembered what really sucked. I stopped walking, indignant. Gesturing at no one in particular, I let loose. "No! What really sucks is that when the developer razes all this Happies land, entire ecosystems are going to be wiped out!" My anger was making me hotter on this already scorching night, and I wished I had one of those ice bricks we kept in the restaurant freezer room for the stray cats to rub along my arms. "Like, did you know there are feral cat colonies living in here?"

"I bet the coyotes adore them."

Ignoring him, I said, "And all these trees. They probably have birds that take cover from the desert sun in them. Birds have nests. All those baby birds, they'll be wiped out."

"And cute little squirrels," Zeke said in a baby voice, mocking me. His overgrown body did a slinky torso dance. "And snakes! Hissss!"

"I'm serious! Nature took back this land after the park closed. Nature deserved it more than we do. But once the developer clears it, the living world inside here will die."

"New trees and animals will come back after the new buildings come up," said Zeke. "That's just the circle of life."

"Why are you so optimistic all the time? It's annoying."

"It's endearing."

"Do you know the moonlight is reflecting on your front pouf? Your hair is like a light beacon."

I reached up to tap the pouf, I don't know why, maybe for luck, but Zeke ducked out of my hand's way. From behind us, perhaps in tribute to Zeke's Prince T-shirt, Jake's voice sang out, *"She's always in my hair."*

Finally, the guy to light *my* fire had arrived.

CHAPTER 18

EZRA AND ESME GET SOME COMPETITION

12 a.m.

"Where've ya been?" Jake asked. "I've been looking for you everywhere."

Zeke said, "I'm right here, obviously."

"Not you, kid," said Jake. He wiggled his index finger in my direction, and damn, that silly gesture on Jake was sexy. "Her. The cute one." His words: sexier.

"I'm fucking cute as hell," said Zeke.

"Yeah, but she has boobs," said Jake. "Cuter."

"How flattering and objectifying," I said.

Zeke said, "Do they have names?"

"Who?" Jake and I both said.

Zeke pointed to his chest, but looked at me. "Your boobs."

I must have been secondhand high from all the marijuana smoke wafting from the miniature golf course installations, because I admitted, "I do have names for them, actually. Ezra and Esme."

Jake said, "Ezra's a guy's name."

"Ezra's the more androgynous one," I said. *Shut up about Ezra and Esme, Vic!* I asked Jake, "Where've you been?"

"I shut down the Chug Bug when the bikers broke down the fence. Decided to follow 'em into the park. I've been trying to text you, but no answer."

My eyes narrowed accusingly at Zeke, who shrugged like, *No big deal.* For a split second, I wondered if he threw my phone specifically so I'd have a harder time finding Jake and my Cuddle Huddle girls. We were having a good time, but Zeke was a friendly dude, and there were plenty of other people in the park whose attention he could monopolize.

We heard the loud, pointed gasp of a lady reaching her apex of pleasure from inside the miniature castle on Lovers Lane. Jake smiled at me. "I told you that place was magic."

"Probably not so sterile, though," said Zeke, suddenly surly.

"Says the boy with the tunneled ears," I said. How quickly could I shake the junior now, and take up residence with Jake in one of these miniature golf coves? Everyone else was doing it. I was tired of being the party monitor. I was ready to be a party fornicator.

"Don't you have your band to set up or something?" said Jake to Zeke. Jake and I were so in sync, eager to get rid of the kid. "Vic and I have some money to count."

BOOM! Another loud sound, but this one didn't belong to the throes-of-ecstasy crowd cavorting in the weeded-over miniature golf course. It came from the liftoff of a fireball into the sky, which exploded, and descended down into Main Street, setting a crumbling building facade on fire.

Mega-Joan wielded a mighty fire extinguisher. "Got it before Bygone Rancho was really bygone. The Wanderlust Hotel is no longer with us. But no good ever came out of that brothel anyway."

She set down the extinguisher and picked up her megaphone again. "DON'T MAKE ME HAVE TO SLAP Y'ALL BACK INTO CLOWN TOWN! WHEN I SAID NO FIRES, I MEANT NO FIRES!"

She nodded to me. Out of breath from running full speed to Main Street from Lovers Lane, I gasped, "Thanks, Joan."

"Who was responsible for this?" Joan asked the party-goers assembled in Bygone Rancho.

A beautiful blond biker chick approached, with another unused fire rocket nestled on her shoulder, wearing shorts so short they barely covered her crotch, cowboy boots, and a tight, vintage, kids' Happies plaid pajama top. She said, "That was me. I couldn't resist. Promise I won't fire any more, Joan." She looked appropriately contrite, and Joan went over and patted her on the shoulder comfortingly.

"I won't throw ya into UnHappies Jail," said Joan. "So long as you keep your promise. Who are ya, darlin'? I don't recognize you."

"Bandita!" said the blond babe, like Mega-Joan should have known.

Mega-Joan said, *"Bandita?* I haven't seen you since you were a Little Miss Happies at the Tulsa off-road convention, what, ten years ago? You sure grew up, Little Missy! How old are you now? Eighteen?"

Mega-Joan placed a kiss on Bandita's cheek, and then buttoned the top button on Bandita's top.

"Twenty-one," Bandita told Mega-Joan.

The air smelled of smoke and tasted like fire, beer, and danger. On the other side of the now burned-down Wanderlust Hotel facade was the UnHappies Jail. I noticed Jake appraising Bandita head to toe with a leering grin, and I wanted to lock the girl into one of the jail cells and throw away the key. Bandita's girls had Ezra and Esme beat. By a lot.

Delroy Cowpoke spoke up next. "My little girl's all grown up, eh, Joan?" The biker dude let out a jolly chortle, like he was a regular Hells Angels Santa Claus.

Zeke stood close to the jail, perhaps intuiting my desire to banish someone into it. Zeke said, "My dad used to tell me about this place. He said it was where people got sent before they were ejected from the park for bad behavior. I always thought he was making it up!"

Delroy said, "Nope, it was for real. Folks got too liquored up—"

"No alcohol was sold on the premises, of course," Mega-Joan interrupted. "Mary Happie never would have allowed that."

Delroy said, "Rules were meant to be broken."

Mega-Joan sighed with disapproval. "People brought in their own hooch. Ernesto Happie designed the original Happies worker vests with a pocket on the inside for cigarettes. He didn't plan on his employees using those pockets to sneak in whiskey flasks to sell to customers."

One of the Happies placed a floodlight on the ground and then stood before us. He was wearing one of the vintage worker vests, covered in Happies patches and pins, and he opened it to reveal the inner pocket. He pulled a flask from the pocket, took a swig, and returned the flask to the pocket, with the skill and flourish of a flight attendant demonstrating emergency procedures.

"What's that vest, a '65?" Delroy asked the Happies vest man.

The vest man scoffed. "Hardly! It's a '62! Certified!" He stepped up close to Delroy and displayed a certificate patch that said " '62" on the inner lining of the vest.

"Fine indeedy," admired Delroy.

"Where's the beer?" asked Bandita.

Jake perked up. "I've got a beer truck nearby and a few craft brews needing some expert taste buds."

Bandita smiled at Jake, liking what she saw. "Pale ale or stout?"

"Malt!" said Jake, and she and Bandita both laughed at some joke I didn't get at all that made me want to bang their two over-gorgeous heads together in beer ignorance frustration. And to make Jake remember I was standing right here.

"Let's go, then," Bandita said to Jake. "I'd love a taste."

"No shenanigans that lead to jail time, darlin'," her father told Bandita.

It was Bandita's turn to roll her eyes. "God, Dad, shut up." She took Jake's hand.

"Didn't we have plans later?" I reminded Jake, trying to sound casual when really what I wanted to say was, *You can't really be propositioning some big-boobed airhead named Bandita, right, Jake? Not when your implied-but-not-committed-to destiny tonight was with* me, *and more average-sized Ezra and Esme?*

Jake winked at me. "Catcha later, cutie," he said to me. And then he took off with Bandita.

My legs felt bolted to the ground, locked in shock. Just like that, Jake was lost to me, chasing another skirt—or, in Bandita's case, a pair of barely-there shorts that just one of my arms probably wouldn't fit into. This night was supposed to end with me and him slapping dollar bills on each other, and doing deeds that could have gotten us sent to the UnHappies Jail, and not him and some biker chick named Bandita with a father named Delroy and what was the matter with people? Did they not know how to name children properly?

Don't throw a party just to impress a guy. I should have heeded my sister's advice. How could this night suck more?

Zeke said, "Uh . . . Vic? Don't freak out, but I just got a text message from Troy Ferguson. Thrope's been spotted, by the Ravishing Ravine."

CHAPTER

19

OOPS, I ANNIHILATED
THE CHUG BUG

1:15 a.m.

Fifteen minutes after Zeke and I found her, the Chug Bug was at the bottom of the Ravishing Ravine. And now Miss Ann Thrope was on the loose.

"I'm putting an end to this party once and for all. It's time to kill all Happies."

Thrope had evil intent but, predictably unreliable, she paused her gun trolling long enough to move the rifle that was cocked on her shoulder (pellet-variety weaponry, we hoped), and she slung it over her back again. The maneuver was apparently to free her hands, because she then took out her phone and placed a call. What the?!?! She had the call on speaker for all to hear, and as soon as a female voice answered the ring, Thrope yelled into the phone, "GET OVER HERE NOW, CHERYL!"

Sheriff Cheryl's voice said, "My wife is fully dilated. YOU deal with it!" In the background, Mayor Jerry's voice could be heard saying, "Push! Push!"

Standing next to me, Zeke quietly sang, *"Ah, push it. Push it real good."*

"This disaster is on you, Cheryl! I'll remember this when *I'm* mayor!" Thrope then let out an epic growl of frustration and ended the call.

Cautiously, I approached her. "Maybe just enjoy yourself now that you're here?" I wasn't being sarcastic. Both our worst fears—Thrope's that the senior class would celebrate a last party at Happies, mine that Thrope would show up to it—had been realized. If Thrope could relax for once, maybe we could all deal—*safely!*—and the party could go on. Yeah, she'd sent the Chug Bug over the ridge, but when the beer supply ran short, everyone would blame me. What was *her* big worry?

Her eyes burned hellfire into mine. "Not maybe. *Will.*" I had no opportunity to experience even a moment of relief, because then she added, "If I can't take this mess down from the outside in, I'll take it down from the inside out."

A Happie from the bus caravan dared to approach her and ask, "Aren't you Miss Happie Annette Thrope?" He reached out his phone for a selfie. Thrope responded by cocking her gun back onto her shoulder and shooting into a nearby tree, successfully dispersing that first wave of Happies trying to surround her.

"I actually think we really do need Sheriff Cheryl," said Zeke.

"I actually think I sort of agree with you." I knew in some way that I should have felt happy—or at least, vindicated. Thrope was finally letting her psycho freak flag wave high for all to see. Instead, I felt panicked—what if she hurt someone?—and hugely guilty about Jake's truck.

Outlaw Thrope stormed off into the darkness, with a second, braver wave of Happies fans following her. If there had been a sound track to Miss Ann Thrope's pace, it would have been the *Wizard of Oz* music when the spinster neighbor lady who became the Wicked Witch of the West rode on her bike to Dorothy's house to take away Toto. Mean, determined, scary as shit.

Like a cavalry coming to the rescue, or a double dose of Glinda the Good Witch sparkling into the scene to save my life, my beautiful bitches finally found me.

"What the fuck happened?" said Fletch as she stared down into the ravine to check out the toppled Chug Bug, whose lights were still beaconing up into the night sky.

"Jake's gonna lose it," said Slick mournfully. "I don't even know what to say."

"Where have you *been*?" I exclaimed. If my girls had been by my side all night, this destruction might not have happened. I would have been partying with them instead of seeking out Thrope. I would have been securing the Chug Bug with them somewhere where it couldn't be pushed into a ravine.

Wishful thinking, I know. But the statistical probability that somehow the altercation with Thrope wouldn't have ended with a totaled Chug Bug at this spot would have been at the very least vastly improved if the Cuddle Huddle had stuck together through the night.

"Where have *you* been?" snapped Fletch. "We've been trying to call you all night."

My eyes shot daggers at Zeke. "Some dumbfuck tossed my phone."

Slick pointed at Zeke. "I've been trying to call you, too!"

"Sorry," said Zeke.

Jake arrived, riding the back of Bandita's motorcycle. He jumped off before she'd even stopped the bike. He saw the beams from the headlights shooting up from the ravine and ran to the side of the ridge where the Chug Bug had been safely parked barely half an hour before. "HOLY SHIT!" he yelled.

We gave Jake a moment to process the shock, and begin the first stage of grief: denial. "No no no. This isn't really happening. It's not possible." He buried his face in his hands.

Slick said, "I'm so sorry, Jake." She tried to place her hands on his shoulders, to comfort him, but he flinched, and shoved her hands away.

Fletch said to me, "This has gone too far. You've gotta end your war with Thrope."

Excuse me? "*Me* end it? She's the one who started it."

Slick turned from futilely trying to comfort her big brother to facing me and saying, "You're the one who provoked it."

"What did I miss?" I asked. My fingers ached—to comfort Jake, and to text my sister so she could tell me how the fuck to handle this situation. "How are you two suddenly on Thrope's side?"

Slick said, "This isn't about sides, Vic! It's not even about you. Look down there. My brother's truck has been destroyed! That thing was his *baby*."

Fletch glanced warily at me, but my eyes were not brave enough to meet hers. She said, "This is serious. It's not a boring Town Council meeting. Thrope's dangerous for real this time. I'm concerned. Maybe we should call the cops. If Sheriff Cheryl won't come, the California Highway Patrol will."

"Don't call CHP!" Jake screeched. "My fucking truck that's now at the bottom of the ravine was serving minors all night. I didn't have a license for the business, and the truck didn't even have insurance or registered plates yet."

Jake dropped to the ground, and the sight was pathetic. He was crying. "I can't believe this. I spent the past year of my life and put every penny I ever had into the Chug Bug. And now it's just . . . gone." Bandita knelt alongside him and massaged his shoulders. He looked up at me. "This is all *your* fault, Vic!"

I couldn't have felt more horrible. "I'm so sorry, Jake."

"The Chug Bug was my ticket out of this stupid town." Jake moaned again. Bandita helped lift him from the ground, and she pulled him to her for a comforting hug. It was like a mandatory symbiosis of the two hottest people in the vicinity, deeply and spiritually connected even if they'd known each other less than an hour.

I was sore that he'd so quickly and casually passed on me in favor of Bandita, but I'd never have wished the truck destruction on him. I said, "I never in my worst nightmare thought Thrope would go so far, Jake. I'll fix the situation, promise. I'll take up a fund tonight to buy you a new VW bus."

My idea fell on deaf ears. "How'd it get all the way over here?" Jake asked us from the other side of Bandita's shoulder.

Slick said, "Fletch and I moved it when we heard Thrope had been spotted. We were trying to help."

Jake said, "So you ruined me."

Fletch said, "We thought we were helping. And don't blame this on us. You knew the risks involved in serving this party."

"Don't be a dick," Zeke said to Jake. "None of us drove the Chug Bug over the ravine."

Jake lifted both his middle fingers to our group. "FUCK YOU ALL!" He released himself from Bandita's grip and said to her, "Let's get out of here. I can't stand the sight of these traitors anymore."

She nodded, and took his hand. They started to walk back toward Bandita's motorcycle, but then Jake let go of her hand, came over, and pointed at me. "Especially you, Vic. I fucking hate you right now. I wish you didn't *exist*."

So. I *could* feel more horrible.

20 WANT MAGIC BURRITO

1:45 a.m.

First Jake abandoned me. Then the Cuddle Huddle mutinied.

A crowd of classmates and some Happies were going down into the ravine to inspect the Chug Bug, totaled and flipped on its rear—it was a crazy sight to behold. The vehicle had not ignited the hillside, and if it hadn't happened by now, it probably wouldn't burn to a crisp after all. That was a small win. But there were so many other fires to extinguish.

Fletch said, "I see Raheem and Emerson down there. I'm gonna go find them. To comfort me." How could she even think about fooling around at a time like this?

Slick said, "I promised Bao Ling I'd collect ribbons with her in Pinata Village to use in her new apartment." And Slick! She was thinking about accessorizing from Happies relics at a time like this?

"But . . ." I sputtered. "But the Cuddle Huddle! We just found each other again and tonight's our last night to be together!" One might think the destruction of a beer truck would be cause for a party to end, but by the excited voices and laughter and more Happies song singing coming from down in the ravine, I'd say the party was just hitting its stride. Thrope's arrival and the bus fiasco had only made the party better.

"Not feeling it," said Fletch.

"*You* aren't feeling it?" I asked them. "*I'm* the one who's mortally wounded here."

"I'm with Fletch," said Slick. "Not feeling it."

The Chug Bug destruction could be directly traced to me spurring Thrope on, but we were all complicit in Jake losing his pride and joy. Usually the Cuddle Huddle stuck together in a crisis. Now, apparently, all bets were off. The downer vibe between us could not be denied.

"Find ya later," said Slick, taking off toward Pinata Village.

"Too much bummer up here. Down into the ravine I go," said Fletch, who then called out, "Raheem! Emerson! Flash me some light so I can see." And she was gone.

Once again, I was left with Zeke. Did this kid not have somewhere else to be tonight? "What the hell did I do to them?" I asked him.

Trying to make me feel better and failing, Zeke said, "You know those Cuddle Huddle girls. Party animals gots to find the party. And it ain't here, obviously."

I sat down on the ground, glum. "A miracle or magic are the only things that could save me tonight."

Zeke looked astounded. "I'd say you *already* got a miracle tonight. Several, in fact."

"How do you figure?"

Zeke sat down alongside me. "Bev Happie authorizing this party. The Happies biker gang arriving and making *an earthquake happen* just to break down the fence to the other side, like they're freaking geologic gods. Then, a beer truck smashed into the bottom of a ravine and managed not to explode! Not great for Jake, but pretty exciting to witness! Want me to go on?"

I smiled a teeny bit, my mood lifting. I lightly nudged my shoulder against his. "Well, maybe some miracles have happened," I allowed. "But there's no magic possible in this dead-end town run by Miss Ann Thrope. God only knows where she's gone by now and what new wave of horror she's unleashing."

"Forget about Thrope for a minute," Zeke said. "Because here, right now, you need to hear it: Magic *is* possible. You just have to believe, bitch." I was too hungry to believe in anything besides the magical power of carbs right now. Just thinking about food made my empty stomach growl, loudly. It wasn't as embarrassing a sound as an outright fart, but it was close. We both laughed. Zeke teased, "I guess someone's tummy is ready for yummies?"

I said, "Make magic happen. Make a burrito appear right now, please?"

"I *wish*. So don't freak out, but I overheard some Happies talking about a cookout happening in the Badlands. I bet we could get some grub there. I mean, if you can shut up for once about fire safety."

"Fuck fire safety. Let's find some food."

I intended to eat my stress rather than cry over Jake, the Cuddle Huddle, or evil Thrope on the warpath. God help Jason Dunker once I found him again because I was going to eat every single brownie he had left, and not pay him, either.

Zeke and I stood up and began walking. I could tell by his slow gait that he was getting tired, and I appreciated that he was sticking by me and trying to keep my spirits high in the face of so much defeat. Zeke asked, "So which one's Esme and which one's Ezra?"

I also appreciated that he was trying to keep me distracted from all the potential disasters playing out in every corner of the Happies land. I laughed and touched my left boob. "This one's Ezra. A little bit smaller than Esme, but trying not to have an inferiority complex about it." *Seriously, Vic. SHUT UP!*

"I noticed that about Ezra, last summer when you were modeling sports bras for me, before you went off to soccer camp. I wasn't going to say anything but now that you've brought it up . . ."

I mock-punched the side of his upper arm. "The push-up bra you recommended worked wonders at soccer camp, by the way."

"Oh, really?" Zeke stopped our walk, stood in front of me, and leaned down to carefully inspect my chest. "You're good luck charms, Ezra and Esme. Keep up the excellent work."

I placed my hand under Zeke's scruffy chin, and lifted his eyes to once again meet mine. "You have way too much interest in boobs for a homosexual." But I didn't mind his curiosity. After the colossal diss from Jake, my wounded ego was soothed by Zeke's flattering attention.

He said, "That's a discriminating assumption. *Everybody* likes boobs. Know what else I love?" Zeke sang a *South Park* song in a deep, sexyman baritone voice. *"Say everybody have you seen my balls? They're big and salty and brown."*

Zeke and his pompadour performed a mad dance around me, and I was a little bit in love with this weirdo man-boy, for keeping me so entertained, and laughing. I might have even kissed him in gratitude, except for the shot that rang off in the distance.

"High holy hell!" Delroy Cowpoke's voice called out.

"UNACCEPTABLE!" Mega-Joan megaphoned.

Zeke and I ran toward the commotion, to the top end of Main Street, where it splintered out into the paths leading to Pinata Village, Lovers Lane, and the Ravishing Ravine. There, we found Delroy and the Happies vintage vest man restraining Annette Thrope, while Mega-Joan unloaded Thrope's rifle.

"Let go of me!" Thrope shouted, viciously squirming.

"What happened?" I asked.

A biker dude Happie pointed to a flagpole sticking up from the back of his bike. The flagpole had a Barbie doll affixed to its top, and the doll wore a pageant gown with a tiara and a Miss Happies sash. "She shot it."

Zeke and I looked more closely. The Miss Happies doll's face had a pellet bullet hole stuck in it, square between the eyes. Damn, Thrope was a good shot. And, major sigh of relief: pellet rifle.

A Happies motorcycle guy opened a vintage Happies "emergency kit" briefcase and tossed a set of handcuffs to Delroy, who snapped the handcuffs around Thrope's wrists behind her back. Then Delroy and the other man led Thrope down Main Street.

Status update: I no longer dreaded the Happies. I fucking *loved* them. Unlike me, they really knew how to handle a party gone too wild. I wanted to cry, the sight of handcuffed Thrope being dragged down Happies' Main Street was so beautiful.

"You can't do this to me!" Thrope shrieked. "Do you know who I am? I practically *own* this town!"

Delroy Cowpoke said, "Not tonight, you don't, darlin'. I won't be having my bikers shot at, even if you ain't packin' real heat. You've left us no choice but to make this citizen's arrest."

He walked Thrope, kicking and screaming, directly into the UnHappies Jail. Mega-Joan lifted her mouthpiece again as Delroy threw Thrope into Happies purgatory. Mega-Joan announced, "Annette Thrope, be advised that Delroy Cowpoke and I are responsible for the safety of our Happies, and we won't have them, or their prized figurines, put in danger. Not even by a former Miss Happies."

"An honor to be shot at by a Miss Happie," the motorcycle dude with the defiled Miss Happie doll said to Thrope as he rode his bike past her in the UnHappies Jail. "But *not cool*."

Delroy took a second set of handcuffs and attached one side to the jail bar in the open-air cell. Then he unlocked Thrope's cuffs, loosened one of her hands, and latched the free side of her cuffs to the second pair to allow her to move around. She was still attached to the jail cell, but at least only one of her hands was bound. The Happies were such compassionate wardens, but Thrope had no appreciation. With her free hand, Thrope took a mighty swing at Delroy, but he ducked just in time. Delroy laughed. "Feisty, aren't you?"

Thrope burned. "I will sue you! Ruin you!"

Delroy said, "You do whatever you need to do tomorrow. Tonight, Happies belongs to the Happies. Just till sunrise, darlin'. Then we'll set you free."

She didn't respond, but glared at me. I wasn't even trying not to gloat. I was thrilled to let my face show it. Thrope sneered, "Enjoy your fun now, Victoria." She paused for dramatic effect, like a teacher about to announce an unnecessarily spiteful pop quiz. "By morning, your besties won't be your besties anymore. It's a promise."

I don't know why I couldn't resist the invitation to engage her. But what could she do to threaten me now that she was locked up in the UnHappies Jail for the night? "Why's that?" I asked, damningly overconfident as usual.

Thrope smirked. "Because I *own* part of your group now. Don't believe me, Victoria? Just ask Mercedes. Your stupid Cuddle Huddle is dead, and you don't even know it."

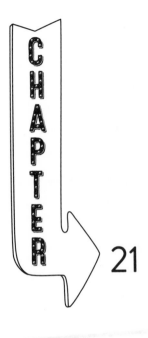

21   BADLANDS: NOT FALSE ADVERTISING

2 a.m.

Elation: Thrope was locked up for the night. Bummed: I'd lost Jake to Bandita (and his fury over the destruction of the Chug Bug). Relief: The Chug Bug hadn't exploded! Unsettled: The weirdness between me, Slick, and Fletch. Sweet: Zeke was still by my side.

My emotions had been bounced around all night like a soccer mom off her antidepressants. With Thrope in UnHappies Jail, at last I thought I might be winning this night (mostly). I was hella tired, but wanting to finally enjoy my own party. I was almost ready to take Zeke's advice to believe in magic, except for the seed of doubt that master manipulator Thrope had planted in my head.

"Do you know what she was talking about?" I asked Zeke as we walked up Main Street toward the Badlands, where a significant contingent of the party had gravitated, at least based on the noise factor and floodlight strobes coming from that direction and the sweet, mouth-watering smell of roasting marshmallows. Fire safety be damned. Gimme gimme gimme. Hungry hungry hungry.

Zeke said, "Thrope? Nope." Pause. "Hey, dope rhyme!"

"Tell that to whoever runs against Thrope for mayor this fall. Perfect slogan. *Thrope? Nope, Dope!*"

"I bet she'll run unopposed."

"True. Being locked up for a night in UnHappies Jail will probably help more than harm her campaign. She'll be like a vigilante hero to the few voters who bother to cast ballots."

I wanted to party. I wanted to *eat*. I wanted to put Thrope's taunt out of my head. But I couldn't. I had to find my friends and figure out what was going on.

"Do you have a signal on your phone?" I asked Zeke.

"I have a decent signal, but only two percent battery power left."

"Please use your remaining juice to text Slick and Fletch and ask them to meet at the Ghost Cemetery?"

"Done."

The legend goes that when the Native Americans and Mexican Army joined forces to slaughter the Union Army who were sleeping on the grounds of what later became Rancho Soldado, the attackers were surprised by an initial line of defense that was of the four-legged variety. The American battalion had traveled with a pack of German shepherds who stood guard at their campsites. The dogs howled, but it was too little warning, too late. The dogs were the first to die. They were the only combatants to receive proper burials. After the savage battle that left the entire American battalion dead, the attackers left the gruesome human remains for the coyotes and wolves, and for the next wave of encroaching Americans to find once searchers reached the site. But the dogs were given respectful burials, in the land that later became the Ghost Cemetery at Happies.

It was a mythological place to any kid in Rancho Soldado, because it was where our parents told us our pets were buried after they were put to sleep at the end of their lives (or when they disappeared). As far as Slick, Fletch, and I knew, the Ghost Cemetery was the final resting ground for the only creatures we loved more than each other: Slick's rabbit, Fletch's doggies, and my turtle. It was a blatantly sentimental choice of meeting place, but I knew they wouldn't question it. They'd show up.

To get there, I first had to go through the Badlands, a fake-engineered area of clay-colored slopes and faux volcanic rock formations. I could smell the roasting marshmallows, but I couldn't locate them, and I was too distracted for a proper search mission.

A mini-party was happening around a former teapot ride that used to tip kids of all ages into fake quicksand. That ride had been my dad's favorite. He used to say the sand was soft and warm and it felt like falling into a heavenly cloud. A Nirvana song blasted from a portable device attached to portable speakers, and people were moshing in the middle of the sand, kicking it, throwing it, jumping in it. Just next to the quicksand, Troy Ferguson was dangling upside down from a tree branch that looked like it was about to break off from his weight, while his drunk friends were egging him to do a backflip into the quicksand: "Swing! Swing!"

Nearby, Olivier Farkas had apparently deposited passed-out Amy Beckerman onto a boulder, leaving him free to threaten Emerson Luong with hostile male shoulder bumps. "You'd better not have given any of those Jell-O shots to Genesis Fletcher, asshole. If those shots were laced with any chemical crap stronger than gelatin, I will personally beat the living shit out of you. Is that why Amy Beckerman is passed out right now? Is it, Emerson?"

Emerson bravely tried to hold his own, but Olivier was like twice his muscle mass. Emerson said, "Amy Becker-barf is passed out because of all the tequila and vodka she mixed into the fucking soft-serve machine, Olivier! And if Genesis would rather hang out with me than you tonight, I promise you the Jell-O shots had nothing to do with it!"

Bold words. Big mistake. Full-on fistfight.

Emerson was out flat in a one-two punch.

Zeke stepped over to Olivier. "Stand down, dude. You win this testosterone round. Now hang back and get some rest."

For a second I feared for Zeke's safety (while applauding his bravery), but then a very exhausted Olivier conceded. "Okay," Olivier grunted, wiping his tired eyes.

Olivier started to head in the direction of Main Street again. "By Amy's side!" I clarified.

Olivier stomped his foot like a whiny child. Then said, "Okay. Fuck."

"First go find some ice for Emerson's face," Zeke told Olivier.

"God you two are bossy!" said Olivier. But he found a Happie with an ice chest, and took it to Emerson, still feebly lying on the ground.

"Let's move on," I said to Zeke. "Quickly."

Zeke and I walked to the other side of the Badlands, dodging spindly cactus trees, 'shrooming classmates, and fornicating Happies (middle-aged people copulating: even grosser than Amy Becker-barf's soft-serve trail). We found Olivier's fellow jocks hanging out by the bumper cars in a field behind the exit to the Badlands. "Epic party, Vic!" cried out Jamila Beshara. She was standing on top of a bumper car turned on its side. Upon closer inspection, almost all the bumper cars in the area were either rolled onto their sides or smashed into each other, and every one of them was covered by grass and weeds. Jamila opened her arms wide to lord over the landscape. "I'm the queen of the world!" she announced with an endearing lack of originality, to cheers from the jocks sitting sideways in the cars.

"Jamila," I called, "I declare you fire marshal for the Badlands for the rest of the night. Unless it involves marshmallows that someone seriously needs to bring me this second, make sure no one tries to start a fire, will you?"

"*Let it go, let it go!*" Zeke the musical Elsa serenaded me. "Just relax already."

"I can't," I said.

"You *can*. You *won't*," said Zeke.

From behind Jamila, Avery Freeman, who'd been voted Pyro Most Likely to Light Up the World at prom, flicked a lighter menacingly. "Hunggrrryyyy," Avery said. "Want fire badly."

Too much booze tonight, too little food to absorb it, just as I'd feared.

I told Zeke, "All these drunk people swinging from trees and swinging at each other. Too many lighters and matches and dumbfucks who probably think they can put a campfire out by just tamping it down with their shirts. No one to run crowd control, no food to soak up the alcohol—"

"Pizza emergency," Zeke interrupted. "I volunteer to make the run."

To be clear, Zeke often invoked pizza emergencies. And while his offer would only address one of my problems, it was a huge help, and I was hugely grateful to the huge-hearted boy. I took my debit card from my wallet and gave it to Zeke. "The PIN is my house number address. Be sure to get a vegan option. Bless you."

"Anything for you, General Navarro," Zeke said. "But just to let you know, I could almost accept a meatless pie, but a cheeseless pizza just breaks my fucking heart." He took off.

"Defy defy defy!" said the voice of Evergrace Everdell, who was lying on her back on top of one of the bumper cars, stargazing next to Bao Ling. Slurring her words, Evergrace said, "I don't accept General Navarro's authority.

I won't adhere to any military industrial complex inside Happies tonight."

Bao Ling suddenly sat up. She raised a beer bottle in salute to me. "Don't mind Evergrace. She had her first beer tonight. She's a little wonky now."

"First *five* beers!" Evergrace said, and hiccupped. She looked at me and then frowned. "The beer hasn't made me fonder of you, Victoria. You still look like an annoying know-it-all. I have no idea why Mercedes clings so hard to you."

"You don't know me, or my friends, so I'd suggest shutting the fuck up," I said to Evergrace. It was silly to argue with a drunk person, but I couldn't not respond to some homeschooled everbitch who had the audacity to challenge my friendships with Slick and Fletch when she'd never even been on school grounds long enough to witness the deep and profound connection I shared with them. *Since kindergarten.*

"*You* don't know your friends," said Evergrace.

Bao Ling said, "I like you, I guess, Vic. But the Cuddle Huddle is old news. A fraud. We're taking custody of Mercedes away from you."

Evergrace said, "We'd snag the other one, too, but she's taking off for Africa."

"I hardly think you're in a position to tell me who my friends are and aren't," I said to Evergrace. But I felt a sense of dread. Something *was* going on, and it seemed like the people I disliked most at this party—Evergrace and Thrope—knew about it.

"I guess you have a nasty surprise coming from the Cuddle Huddle," said Evergrace.

And then she puked on my shoes.

22 R.I.P. CUDDLE HUDDLE
2:30 a.m.

The Happies caravan supply machine had clearly passed through the Ghost Cemetery long before I arrived. There were portable standing lanterns randomly placed throughout, with flickering candles inside them that lit my way as I walked. The lighting was a nice touch. Why didn't I ever travel with candles on hand for impromptu cemetery nights?

Mary and Ernesto Happie had reportedly buried their own family's pets in the Ghost Cemetery. I saw that their tradition had been carried on long after the theme park was closed, as I trampled across grave markers with dates inscribed within the past few years, and referencing pet names that would not have been likely during the Happies park era.

RIP, YEEZUS-DOG. YOU WERE A #SMITHFAMILYBLESSING.

FURREVER IN OUR ♥ S, KITTY GAGA.

WE'LL ALWAYS LOVE YOU, TAYLOR NOT-SWIFT.

My turtle! Dear, sweet Taylor Not-Swift! She died soon after Mom left. I never really believed Dad had buried her here, but he had!

I'd spent most of my life believing the Happies theme park was a forbidden place, where only graffiti artists or drunken kids trespassed, but it was clear to me now that many people had been coming through here, and often. Even my dad! Maybe this was where he'd gone to mourn, or just be alone, when being Mr. Mom got to be too much for him.

Why had I been such a coward to never come see this place for myself? I promised myself I'd be more adventurous in the future. A trespasser. Fearless. Lighting my own way and not waiting on others to do it ahead of my arrival.

The Happies Ghost Cemetery was organized like a miniature golf course where you went from hole to hole, but instead of fake castles and moats, you passed through headstones, mausoleums, and benches where a person could sit and ponder life, death, and whether that overconsumption of Happies' burgers, fries, milk shakes, and RASmatazz pies was going to forcibly come out of your mouth or your butt. I nearly tripped over a plaster cast of a giant gypsy woman's head, tipped on its side. Some smart-ass had painted a thin stream of blood from the side of her mouth. I assumed the head belonged to Madame Svetlana, the once glass-encased, animatronic fortune-teller who predicted the death dates of generations of morose Happies seeking her counsel. Just past Madame Svetlana, I spotted the backs of Fletch and Slick, sitting on a small boulder.

There was finally a little wind, noticeably cooling the air, but it wasn't strong enough to account for the loud howling noises emanating from an unknown location within the cemetery perimeter. Were these grounds truly haunted? As a *whoosh* of white noise felt like it cut through my body, I could definitely be counted as a believer. "Hey!" I called to Fletch and Slick. I was as frightened to face them as I was by the howling, and the knowledge that I was traipsing on sacred burial ground.

Evergrace Everdell didn't know what she was talking about. The homeschooled girl was a known anarchist. What could she possibly know that I didn't about my most important friendships? I reached my BFFs and stood in front of them. I said, "Evergrace Everdell, of all people, said you have some big news for me." *Why am I hearing that from her first?* I didn't say. This whole situation was so stupid. Really what I should have been announcing was the amazing discovery of Taylor Not-Swift's final resting place.

Fletch wrinkled her nose. "Have some buried animals risen from the dead? You smell like you just stepped through dog shit."

I said, "No. Evergrace Everdell barfed on my shoes. But thanks for the warm welcome."

Fletch said, "That Evergrace is full of surprises tonight, for a girl who never showed up to school except for extracurricular activities."

"Everbitch also owes me fifty bucks for a new pair of shoes," I said.

Fletch said, "She could get you paid, because guess what? She's got a job now. Wait'll you hear this one."

Fletch looked accusingly at Slick, who then looked guiltily at me. Slick said, "I just finished telling Fletch. I'm moving to Las Vegas."

Yeah. Okay. This was good news for Slick, I supposed, but it didn't feel like a big reveal, either. With Slick's typical laziness, it could take months, or years, before Slick evolved out of her basic inertia and got past the idea to actually moving to Las Vegas. Like, with all her stuff, and not just going there for a quick trip to see if her fake ID worked at the Bellagio hotel bar.

"That's awesome," I said, trying to be encouraging. "You should try new places. You don't always have to be stuck here."

Fletch said, "Oh, she's definitely not stuck here."

Oh, Slick had a reveal alright. She announced: "I got an apartment. My parents cosigned it last week. The lease starts first of July. I'm going to be roommates with Bao Ling and Evergrace Everdell. Thrope helped us get hotel jobs."

"WHAT?" I yelled.

"Right?" said Fletch to me.

I felt beyond betrayed. Slick must have known for a long time about these plans, and she'd never once given so much as a hint. A huge part of her life had played out over the past few months without her including us in any of it, and aided and abetted by Public Enemy Number One: Thrope.

I said, "It's like you want to cut us out of your life."

"Because I have other friends?" Slick asked. "That's absurd—"

"No," Fletch interrupted. "Because you didn't include us in any stage of this big plan. It's like you've been leading a double life. What you do with us—"

"And everything else," I finished.

"That's because I don't trust you two!" Slick let out.

There was a stunned silence, broken only by deeper

howling noises coming up from the ravine. I couldn't imagine how Slick could have hurt us worse.

"You don't trust *us*? What did *we* do?" Fletch finally said, very low and calm, which meant she was on the verge of eruption. Traditionally the steadiest member of our group, Fletch also had the most volatile temper once her calm reached its tipping point.

Slick held up her phone and hit play on a video on the screen. "I found this on Jake's phone and sent it to mine." Fletch and I looked closely. It was a montage of images from the Happies restaurant security cameras. There was Jake, flirting with pretty, besotted girls at the cashier booth. There was Jake, feeling up the attractive lady who delivered the produce to Happies every morning, in the back parking lot. There was Jake, making out with Fletch on the *DDR* platform in the game room. There was Jake, with me, in the freezer room, about to . . .

"I think we've seen enough," said Fletch. She took the phone from Slick and closed the video application. Fletch and I shared a disgusted look: Jake had no respect for others' privacy, he had an outsized ego, and he was a perv.

"I'm sorry, Slick . . ." I started to say.

"Mercedes!" Slick interrupted. "My name is Mercedes! I'm sick of being called 'Slick.' It's not that clever a name, I'm not that clumsy, and I don't like it."

If that's what she was most mad about, we were going to be okay.

"Fine," said Fletch. "Mercedes."

"Does this mean we can't call you 'Fletch' anymore?" I asked Genesis Fletcher. There were more important matters to discuss, obviously . . . but were there really? Our whole friendship identity felt cemented in our names for each other.

Fletch said, "I don't really care. It's *your* name for me. I'm fine with that. Everywhere else, I'm Genesis." She didn't say, *I like that.*

Slick—I mean, Mercedes, said, "Excuse me, I think you two lost sight of the real problem here. Do you dumbsluts have anything to say for yourselves and your betrayals— emphasis plural? Because you *both* did my brother?"

"Everybody does your brother," Fletch said, gentle but informative.

"I know! That's exactly why you two shouldn't have!" said Mercedes.

I was a little bit less guilty than Fletch, it should be noted. "I didn't . . . all the way," I said, a coward trying to cover her very exposed ass.

"Wait a minute," said Fletch. "You're being hypocritical, *Mercedes.* You're trying to dodge the real issue."

"I am not!" said Slick. Damn it, *Mercedes*!

"Why's she hypocritical? What's the real issue?" I asked.

Mercedes rolled her eyes, and then said to me, "Fletch thinks I shouldn't care about you guys being with Jake. Because I lost my virginity to Chester."

"WHAT?" I screamed, this time so loud I was sure my voice echoed across the ravine.

"See?" said Mercedes. "How's *that* feel?"

"Shocking!" I said. First there was the shock of, *Ew, one of my best friends slept with my brother!* Second was the shock of, *My brother got some from a hot girl?* "How did that even happen? When? You said you lost your virginity to Nestor Castillo!"

"Well, I guess I lied," said Mercedes. "It was Chester, and it was while you were away at soccer camp last summer." I was never, ever going to soccer camp again, because apparently everything interesting happened while I was away.

I said, "So did you guys go out? Was it a relationship? I don't understand!"

"It was curiosity," admitted Sli . . . *Mercedes.* "Just that one time. Random. There was so much unnecessary anticipation over doing the deed for the first time. For me, it was just something I wanted to get over with." She sounded so casual about such a major thing. I would have felt bad for

Chester except then she added, "And your brother is so sweet. He made me breakfast the next morning."

I was a dumbfounded dumbslut. "Your definition of sweet romance is that Chester made you Froot Loops for breakfast after?"

"Waffles! And they were fucking delicious! He made a delightful apple compote on top!"

"Chester doesn't cook!" I was seriously ready to punch *Mercedes* in the face. And I'd never, ever felt that way about Slick.

Mercedes said, "Yes, he does! Just not for *you*!"

Whoa, what had just happened here?

"You're just using Chester and Jake to dodge the real issue!" Fletch shouted. "That you backstabbed us with Evergrace Everdell and Bao Ling!"

"YEAH!" I affirmed.

Then Fletch turned her wrath on me. "And *you*, Victoria Navarro! It's your fault that I'm going to Africa tomorrow when I *totally don't want to go*!"

"What? Why?" Mercedes and I both said, nearly forgetting that Fletch had just personally attacked us, because why wouldn't she want to go to Africa when she'd spent the past few months so diligently preparing, and the past few years emotionally committing to returning to her birth nation?

Fletch said, "I want to be frivolous and, like, wander around Europe. I want to wake up hungover in youth hostels and not know where I'm going or what I'm doing. I want to kiss strange boys with funny accents, and be completely selfish."

"So go do that!" I challenged her.

"We're not holding you back," said Mercedes.

Fletch pointed at me. "Because *you*! You're always holding me up as this standard. The Smartest. The Most Politically Committed. It's like you created this identity of intellect and sacrifice for me that now I'm stuck living."

Mercedes picked up on this accusation and pointed at me as well. "Yeah, Vic. You totally do that. You created this identity for me that's all 'Oh, Slick is so lazy, she's so klutzy, she's so lost and incompetent.'"

"I never said that!" I said.

"It's the vibe you give out," said Mercedes. "You cast people in roles and then expect them to live it."

I didn't think that was true about me at all, but I was too hurt and insulted to defend myself, so I turned it on them.

"At least I don't take favors from Miss Ann Thrope," I said to Slick. "You act like you hated her all this time but you were just another one of her pawns in her power-mad game to rule Rancho Soldado."

Slick's-Not-Her-Name said, "Thrope's genuinely mean, but she's not that bad once you get on her good side. She's just another person you created a one-dimensional role for."

Thrope's not that bad once you get on her good side. Who'd be so soulless to *try* to get on Thrope's "good" side?

My former best friend had allied herself with, and was defending, my worst enemy. My other former best friend had accused me of sabotaging her secret desire to be an epic goof-off, like it was my personal responsibility that she chose African aid work over European booty calls.

"Fuck you," I said to them both.

"Fuck *you*," they said back.

I thought I knew my friends, but they had turned into people I didn't know at all. Monsters. Worst of all, they thought *I* was the monster.

There was nothing for me to do but leave them.

So, I ran.

Cuddle Huddle dismissed. Forever.

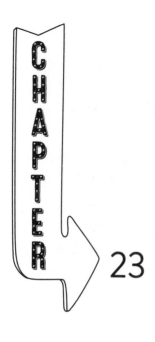

23

CHESTER, THE NEW
LINDSAY

3 a.m.

I ran back across the Ghost Cemetery until I reached the
outskirts of Pinata Village. I didn't know where to wander and I was too hungry and betrayed to think straight.
So, as usual, I defaulted to where Lindsay wanted me to
go, the same methodology I'd used when I didn't get into
USC and decided to move to San Francisco instead.

Was my methodology flawed? Should I have explored
other options besides what Lindsay said I should do?
At this point I was questioning every damn decision I'd
ever made in my life, particularly my sucky choices of
BFFs and my male lust target. Stupid Jake. Stupid Chug
Bug. Stupid Cuddle Huddle. Stupid night. Stupid mythic

roasted marshmallows that never found their way into my mouth.

Out of breath, exhausted, emotionally destroyed, and starving, I sat down on a cracked wooden bench in the outlying area of the village for some rest. I needed to not talk to anyone for a while. I needed to send psychic signals to Zeke to bring me some pizza *now*. And then let me eat in silence.

"Are you hiding?" I heard a voice ask me. I had closed my eyes and was about to fall asleep, into a welcome new consciousness where I wasn't responsible for so many debacles. I didn't want to return to a wakeful state, but the voice was sweetly familiar, like Dad's.

"Yes," I murmured. My eyes blinked open and I saw Chester staring at me intently, concerned, as if he was about to check my forehead for a fever.

"Should I leave you alone?" Chester asked.

"No." I sat up. It was probably the first time in my life my brother's goofball face was so welcome.

"Lindsay's freaking out," said Chester. "She's been texting you all night and not getting answers."

"I lost my phone."

"She was ready to call in the Missing Persons Unit. You're sure gonna have fun living with that neurotic nightmare in San Francisco."

"Don't speak about your sister that way."

"I speak truth." I knew Chester was right. I adored Lindsay, but she also wanted to know where I was every second of the day, like she was my mom. Our real mother lived thousands of miles away and checked in occasionally, but truthfully, Mom didn't seem all that worried or concerned about us. And maybe because she didn't, Lindsay felt she had to. Maybe Lindsay didn't need to anymore.

"Hey," I said. It had never occurred to me before but suddenly I asked Chester, "Do you think I should go live with Mom in Montreal for a little while? I could learn French and . . ."

Chester shook his head. "Absolutely not. We're Southern Californians. We fear cold." I suspected he meant Mom's coldness as much as he meant the northern climate. I suspected my brother was sort of trying to protect me.

I said, "San Francisco is cold, and Lindsay manages fine."

"That's because her veins are made of ice."

I smiled, despite my pissy mood. "You hate that you love and worship Lindsay so much."

Chester said, "No, *you* hate that you love and worship her so much."

"I don't hate it. I fully acknowledge it."

"Repress it," said Chester. "Much healthier."

I laughed. "What are you doing here?"

"Checking in on you, obviously." Chester offered no further information so I raised my eyebrow at him, like, *Come on*. Finally, he admitted, "Lindsay said I couldn't leave tonight until I found you and got you home safely and sent her a text showing you asleep in your own bed."

It was a sweet and caring demand on Lindsay's part, but also a giant red flag about what it would be like to live with her. Would I never be allowed a night out carousing the city without my sister helicopter-parenting me the whole time? Dad and Chester were way more mellow housemates than my sister. If I was a neurotic, controlling person, it was largely because I learned it from Lindsay, the master. I loved my sister and would be forever grateful for the safety net she'd provided after our mom left, but was moving into her group house really such a good plan? If I'd learned anything from this night, it was that my spontaneous ideas had too much possibility for disaster. I had literally gotten the rejection from USC on April 15, and on April 16 I told my sister I needed to move somewhere, anywhere—and she said I should move in with her until I figured things out. If my sister says I should do it, I do it. (Except when I don't. Like when she told me to apply to schools other than USC, and I didn't. Like when she told me not to throw a party to impress a guy. And here I was.)

Was I doing it because it was the right thing to do, or to appear confident and decisive about my self-made lack of options?

"This night sucks," I said. "And I can't leave until the Happies and all my classmates have left the premises."

"Sure you can," said Chester. He paused and then added, "Although you'd be a jerk if you did."

He sat down on the creaky bench next to me, and said nothing more, seemingly content to look up at the stars in the sky. After a few minutes of silence between us, I said, "If Lindsay were here now, she'd tell you that you need to, like, comfort me. Make me feel better."

"Why?" said Chester.

"Because I'm upset."

"About what?"

Grr, men! Clueless clueless clueless. "Um, the Chug Bug was destroyed. Did you hear?"

"I heard. Sucks. Hard." His voice barely registered emotion, and the Chug Bug had been almost as much a labor of love for Chester as it was for Jake.

"Jake said he wished I never existed."

"Harsh."

"Do *you* wish I never existed?"

"Only when you leave the toilet seat down."

"So, like, a lot."

"Yeah. But it's an irritated hate. I wish a second bath-room existed in our house more than I wish *you* didn't exist."

"Thank you, brother."

"But not by much," he amended.

So many other worries fluttered through my troubled mind. "Bev Happie is probably going to kill me when she arrives in the morning to close the real estate sale. Did you know the Happies locked up Annette Thrope?"

"Yup. Saw her on my way here, cuffed to the jail cell. It was beautiful. Maybe the best thing that's ever happened in Rancho, even if she did promise as I walked by her that she was going to make every day in the future a living hell for the Navarro family."

"I wasn't even the one who locked her up!"

"But you were the one who threw the party that got the people who locked her up here."

I ignored his logic and said, "Just like her to hold me accountable, and not the people who did it to her."

Chester showed no emotion or concern and offered exactly no advice about Thrope's jailhouse threat. He just said, "No worries."

Perhaps there is some benefit to subsisting on a diet

of Froot Loops and marijuana. It gives a person no legitimate cares in the world.

"You're being a very bad Lindsay substitute," I told him. "You're not helping me at all."

"You're being too good a Lindsay," he answered. "Telling me what to do and then telling me how badly I'm doing it."

Ouch. "Sorry," I said. I figured I owed him full disclosure of all the night's suckage, so I gave him the other piece of bad news. "Slick and Fletch—I mean, Mercedes and Genesis, I guess—and I just had a huge fight and I don't know if we're really friends anymore."

Finally, he had an actual human, non-Vulcan reaction. "*Whoa!*" Chester declared. "That *sucks*."

"Thank you for acknowledging my pain."

"The other problems will work themselves out. But the friend one, you need to fix. You need to make it right before it's too late, before Fletch leaves."

"They insulted me, attacked me, *lied* to me! Why should I be the one to find them and make up?"

"Because they're your heart," said Chester, as if it was just that simple.

I had to pause our conversation to suck in a wave of oxygen shock. There was a lot more depth to my brother than I'd realized. After taking a few seconds to absorb this revelation, and a moment of frustration that I didn't have my phone available to text Lindsay about it *immediately*, I said, "So you and Mercedes, huh?"

"Aw," was all Chester said back, giving me no clue whatsoever about whether the dalliance had been meaningful to him.

I was deprived of the opportunity to dig deeper into the topic when my head was, once again, bonked with a barrage of marshmallows.

"Evergrace Everdell, where are you?" I fumed. I was too mad at her to actually eat one of the marshmallows tainted by her touch. But damn how I wanted to.

Evergrace emerged from behind a tree next to the bench where Chester and I sat. She burped. "Right here."

"Back away from my shoes," I warned her.

Chester kicked some sand onto my feet. "That'll help the stink," he said.

"Doubt it," taunted Everbitch. I couldn't believe that Slick—ugh, *Mercedes*—was friends with this person, much less that they were going to be actual roommates and start new lives together in Las Vegas. "Have you talked with Mercedes? Bet you're sorry you didn't invite me to this party now!"

"It should be obvious by now why I didn't invite you!"

Evergrace said nothing in response, but dared to shoot another marshmallow at me. I stood up from the bench I'd been sharing with Chester, walked over to her, took the marshmallow rifle from her hands, and said, "If you fucking shoot another marshmallow tonight, I will . . . eat your entire remaining supply!"

"Jealous!" Evergrace squealed. "You're so jealous of me, aren't you?"

"Hardly!"

"It's okay, you don't have to admit it. I can see it all over your face. You tried to have me excluded from this party. Ever since I moved to Rancho Soldado, any time I tried to be friends with you and your stupid clique, you totally dismissed me."

Chester said, "To be fair, Vic dismisses *everyone* who tries to get inside her clique. There's them, and there's everyone else. It's not personal."

"Thank you?" I said to Chester.

Evergrace started to sway a little, and Chester and I surrounded her on either side, each of us taking one of her arms to steady her. "Sleep now?" said Evergrace. Her body went limp as her eyes fluttered closed.

She passed out, into Chester's arms. I didn't want to touch that beast, but I couldn't leave my brother hanging like that, so I helped him place her on the ground. She was in no real danger if we left her there for a while. She just needed a good slap. I mean, sleep.

"That was interesting," said Chester over her dozing body.

I should have left it at that, but like a regular Lindsay, I had to offer unsolicited commentary. "For a guy who's baked most of the time, you're pretty together."

Chester said, "I don't smoke nearly as much weed as you and Lindsay have decided I do, with little to no evidence to back up your assumptions besides the occasional stash in my room, and because I rarely have that much to say. Know why? Mostly because you two never shut the fuck up."

I kissed my brother's cheek. "I love you, bro-man."

"You too. Are you sure you really want to move to San Francisco?"

"What, do you want me to be your housemate longer?"

"I don't care either way. But if you don't have a job or school already lined up there, what's the rush to leave? Your soul seems pretty rooted here."

"You're fucking with my head."

"Get out of your own way," Chester advised. "Now go find the Cuddle Huddle, make it right. And please, if you really do love me, make it so I never have to say the words 'Cuddle Huddle' again."

As we started walking back toward the partying crowds, I noticed a truck now parked at the entrance to Pinata Village. It was a food truck. Someone was handing out plates of food and bottles of water.

I should have rejoiced. Instead, I said, "Oh shit."

"What's wrong?" asked Chester.

I hadn't thought it was possible, but a more fearsome threat than Thrope loomed.

I said, "Parents."

24

TACO'CLOCK: BETTER LATE THAN NEVER

3:30 a.m.

I'm a vegetarian, but I still couldn't resist.

I had to face those parental animals sometime. I might as well do it over some of their amazing chopped tortillas fried in eggs, oil, onion, garlic, and topped with Korean BBQ.

I went to the front counter of the Mexican Seoul food truck, to the side of the long line waiting for food. Selena Zavala-Kim saw me. She called to me, "What'll it be, General I'm-Pretty-Peeved-With-You Navarro?"

There was no point acting affronted. I was too hungry to bother. "Those *chilaquiles* everyone's eating look pretty good."

Selena dished me a plate. "The tofu BBQ, sriracha on the side?"

"As always, thank you."

She handed me a steaming-hot plate of meat-free chilaquiles and a bottle of sriracha from below her counter. I tried to step away, but she said, "Park your legs right there, young lady." Then, while handing out plates to partygoers desperately in need of drunk food, she went into major mom mode. "Not happy with you, Victoria Navarro. Wanna know how we ended up here?" I shook my head but she continued on anyway. "We were supposed to cater the late-night after-party of a posh wedding, but the wedding got canceled. Not even at the last minute. *During.* Bride got cold feet during the sunset ceremony. Seriously! Standing there, barefoot on the beach, fanciest hotel in Laguna, she just dropped her bouquet and said, 'I don't.' It was hard to tell if her family was more infuriated or relieved. Her parents paid us, and we said of course we'd stay to feed their guests, but they said we should donate the food."

"Nice of them," I said between grateful bites.

"You've got sriracha dripping down your chin, honey. Here's a napkin. So, Jon and I were planning to stay overnight in Orange County anyway. But then our phones started to go off with messages about a party happening to celebrate the last night at Happies. We had all this excess food, so we thought, why not bring taco'clock there as a surprise."

"Great idea," I exclaimed. *Except for the surprise part.* Parents should never, ever surprise like that.

"Agreed. We're awesome that way. Then there was a bad accident on the 15; we sat in that mess for nearly two hours. We almost considered not coming at all, we were so tired. But Jon and I decided, 'Of course we should help celebrate! I mean, last night at Happies! Let's be there for our kids! Even when the little shits can't be bothered to answer our many text messages.'" Her voice turned increasingly sardonic, her expression irritated. "So we make that long drive back from OC and stop home to pick up more water bottles from the basement, because we thought you guys would need the hydration, partying out here in the desert in the middle of the night." Long pause, like she was waiting for me to admit guilt. When none came, she said, "How *interesting*, then, that all the cases of beer were missing."

I swallowed. God, best chilaquiles of my life.

I confessed. "My idea. I'm to blame. We were going to replace all the cases in the morning." The Z-K kids would catch plenty of flack from their parents for being in on the scheme, but I wanted Selena to know I was the prime instigator.

"It's not about the beer being replaced, and you know

it. If you think I would have authorized the beer supply going to the entire graduating class of minors at Rancho Soldado High, you'd be wrong."

"Sorry," I said. Was now a bad time to also ask for a side order of kimchi tacos, hold the kimchi, extra everything else? "Really, really sorry, Selena. It's all my fault."

A motorcycle rode by slowly, driven by Bandita, with Jake holding on to her from behind.

"Jake!" Selena called to him. "Get off that bike and get over here *now*."

The motorcycle stopped, but Jake did not get off.

Zeke had also arrived at the same time, carrying a load of pizzas. To him, Selena said, "Help Daddy, please. I need to speak with your brother."

Zeke dropped the pizzas onto the ground and called out, "Free for all!" The stragglers at the end of the Mexican Seoul line swarmed the pizzas, while Zeke stepped inside his parents' food truck. Selena handed him her apron. He put it on and stepped into her place to serve food like a pro. I was so jealous of the guy who'd be lucky enough to win Zeke's heart. He was the real star in the Z-K male progeny gene pool, not stupid handsome Jake with the hidden cameras and the slut tendencies.

I watched as Selena stormed over to Jake. "Do you understand the liability you've exposed us to?"

Jake said nothing.

Bandita stepped up to defend Jake like she'd known him for years instead of a few hours. "He was going to pay you back for the beer."

Selena silenced her with a wave. "Please stay out of it. I don't even know who you are."

Jake finally spoke up. He told his mother, "It was all Vic's idea. To borrow from your beer supply and replace it in the morning before you got home."

Thanks, rat.

Selena already knew what Jake had just told her, but I wanted her to know that my own selfish interests notwithstanding, I'd been trying to help Jake, too. "It's true. My stupid scheme. I wanted to help Jake get exposure for the Chug Bug." I looked to Jake, foolishly wishing he'd jump in at any time to take some responsibility. He did not. "I'm so sorry, Selena. I didn't really consider your liability when I proposed the idea. I'm an idiot." *Jake's a bigger one*, I didn't add.

Selena looked to Jake. "Any apologies in there from you, too?"

Jake shrugged. "I just did it to help Vic. So she could be the big shot who got beer for the party." He glared at me.

"Don't lay it all on me!" I said to him. "You were equally complicit. *You* wanted to be the beer hero just as much. And reap the cash rewards."

Bandita jumped in again. She told Selena, "He did! Show her the money, Jake. He has piles and piles of it!"

Jake took out the beer money box stored inside Bandita's motorcycle trunk, and tossed it to Selena like it was a crayon box and not a cash box holding thousands of dollars.

Holy shit, Jake had stored away the money before leaving the beer truck! The Chug Bug might have been destroyed, but at least the ravine hadn't also swallowed its profits. Phew! We could pay back Selena and Jon for the supply we'd illicitly "borrowed."

Selena caught the metal box. I really wanted to know how much was in it, just to know how profitable my scheme had been, but the look of abject fury on Selena's face held me back from asking. "If some drunk kids at this party had gotten into an accident, or worse, this could have cost us our business," she said to Jake, holding up the box.

It seriously had never occurred to me that the Z-K parents and their business, their lifeline, could potentially be held accountable like that. I felt awful. To Selena, I said, "Sometimes my schemes are good . . . but not so well thought out. I'm so, so sorry."

"Thank you," Selena said to me, curt but at least acknowledging my apology.

"Can we talk about this later, Mom?" said Jake. "Privately." The argument had become an accidental sideshow, with party people lingering around, listening, while slurping up chilaquiles and short-rib tacos. That might have been the end of it, except then he added, "It wasn't *that* big a deal. Losing my Chug Bug was much worse."

That did it. Selena threw the metal box back at him, hitting his arm, hard. "Keep it," she spat. "You'll need it to find your own place. No more living rent-free at Mommy and Daddy's. We can't be crutches to your arrested adolescence anymore." Then, she started yelling at him in Spanish, which meant she was not just pissed. She was hellfire mad. My Spanish is so-so, but the gist of it was: "You ungrateful little lothario. I'm glad your beer truck was destroyed because you'll make a terrible businessman. You don't care about anybody beside yourself. I love you, baby. But it's time for you to be your own man. And you'd best leave soon, before I personally strangle you here and now in front of all these people and your latest conquest."

Selena gave an excellent rant. And that was just the parts I understood.

Then she returned to the Mexican Seoul truck, and slammed the door behind her. She'd said her piece. She was done.

"You suck, Jake," I said to him. "Your little brother is

way more a man than you are, you know that?" I thought of Zeke, who tried to stand up for me earlier to the Happies biker gang, who kept trying to take responsibility for my messes, who had helped and encouraged me at every turn tonight. "And you're a coward. Getting kicked out of your house is probably the best thing that could happen to you. You wanted to leave Rancho so bad? Go."

"I suck?" Jake taunted me. "You're the suck-up."

"At least I take responsibility for my actions." I looked to Bandita. "Please, take him. He's all yours! And *good luck.*"

Good riddance.

Chester walked over to Jake, for what I assumed would be a last good-bye. But there was no tender hug. Instead, Chester pointed his index finger and shoved it into Jake's chest with each of the choice words he had for Jake. "Don't you ever say you wish my little sister didn't exist. Only Lindsay and I get to say that, and that's because we don't mean it."

"You're a horrible mechanic," Jake said to Chester, in a half-teasing tone of voice, like he was at least trying to salvage his friendship with Chester with mocking bro-banter.

"I was never trying to be a good one," said indifferent Chester. "And that fedora you always wear for the chicks is stupid as shit."

To prove Chester's point, I lifted the fedora directly off Jake's head, threw it to the ground, and stomped all over it.

The fedora-smashing was the last straw.

Jake stormed off to Bandita's motorcycle, his new girl in tow.

Chester placed his arm around my shoulder. Navarros stick together. I said to him, "You've always been his wingman. I would have guessed you'd want to follow him. Don't you want to fly free, see the world, carve out your fortune in the great beyond?"

Chester said, "Nope. I'm content here. And having ambition is overrated. Because then you have to live up to it. When you don't have it, you can actually enjoy life for what it is. Simple."

"That's deep, Yoda."

"Welcome, you are," said Chester.

Jake had just settled onto the seat of Bandita's motorcycle when Zeke ran over to him, pulling me along. "Apologize to her," said Zeke to his big brother.

Jake stepped off the bike. "Don't do this, little man," he said to Zeke. "She's not worth it."

"She is!" said Zeke, who then shoved his brother so hard that Jake fell over. Serious wrestling ensued. Chester ran over and tried to pry them apart while Bandita and

I regarded the tussle with satisfaction; she for Jake, me for Zeke. "I said, apologize to Vic!" Zeke repeated to Jake, pinning him to the ground, about to deliver a punch to the jaw. "Own up to your decisions like a man!"

To my shock, Jake gave in. I'm not sure if it was because he knew his little brother was big enough to beat the shit out of him now, or because he didn't want to hurt his brother by continuing to try pummeling Zeke, or he just wanted to go already, and be done with this party, and with Rancho. "Sorry," Jake mumbled in my direction, insincerely, not making eye contact with me.

I had no response. There was nothing to say. Everything about Jake as I'd known him was over.

Zeke let go and Jake stood up. Not acknowledging any of us, Jake hopped back onto the back of Bandita's motorcycle, and the two of them rode off into the darkness.

I knew it would be a long time before Rancho Soldado saw Jake Zavala-Kim again. And that was probably for the best for him, and the security-cam privacy rights of Rancho's nubile female population.

Chester said, "I need some quesadillas to smooth out all this emotional turbulence." Chester deserted us to return to the Mexican Seoul line.

———

Once again left with Zeke, I turned to him. I should have been thankful, but I was annoyed. He could have really gotten hurt in that brawl. It was sweet of him, but I didn't need him defending me. I could take care of myself. We both had so much pent-up energy and now I wanted to expend some on him. "What the fuck was that?" I asked him. "I had no idea you were so . . ." I was about to say "strong," but before I could finish, Zeke grabbed me to him. His mouth moved dangerously close to mine, and I scrunched my lips like, *What the hell?* Then, really what the hell, because Zeke's lips were on mine, moist and firm and electric, completely unscrunching mine with the hottest, most unexpected kiss of my eighteen years so far on earth.

I didn't want the kiss to end, ever, but Zeke pulled back and said, "You had no idea I was so passionate?"

"Yeah," I whispered, still in shock. "And straight?"

"I never said I was gay. You just assumed it."

"You never corrected me!"

"I wanted you to figure it out for yourself. I didn't think it would take you so long that I'd have to fucking show you!" I tugged him back to me, pressing my cheek against his broad chest and grabbing onto the chub on either side of his waist. This boy-man had so much deliciousness to cling to. I couldn't wait to grab on to more, and more, and more. Fuck yeah!

Zeke placed his index finger beneath my chin and lifted my gaze to meet his. He smiled, his multicolored Mohawk like a beacon of encouragement over his kind brown eyes. Even his chunnel ears were suddenly appealing. I responded by standing on tippy-toes and placing my hands on his cheeks. His lips parted, and I lunged for them, the sweetest mouth mine had ever met. This time the kiss was alternately slow and fast, exploratory but eager. Fully heterosexual. Full of surprise and promise.

His hand barely grazed Esme, and I pulled back and smacked his cheek. An angry yet affectionate slap—not too hard, not too soft. Just right. "Last summer! You let me model bras for you because you knew I thought you were gay."

Zeke half-smiled. "Your mistake," he said. "My free show. It was *awesome*." He bowed to my boobs. "Thank you, Ezra and Esme."

Then he pulled me back to him for yet another delirious kiss.

"Dudes," said a voice from behind us. Zeke and I separated and saw Jason Dunker, holding a pizza box. "No one touched the vegan pie."

"So don't eat it," I advised the Dunk, thinking this was obvious.

"I bet Thrope's hungry," said the Dunk.

"It *is* the lowest carbs option," I said, feeling generous

"Shall I feed the prisoner?" the Dunk asked.

"Please do."

The Dunk said, "Did you hear the message she wrote in pebbles in her jail cell?" Zeke and I shook our heads. The Dunk laughed. *"Surrender Victoria."*

It was a good one, I had to give her that.

Zeke said, "I forgot to ask for mushrooms when I ordered the pizzas. Maybe add one on her slice."

CHAPTER 25

TOWN SOCIAL IN
PINATA VILLAGE

4 a.m.

Somehow the raging party had not burned beyond control, and I'd kissed a cute boy, and pretty damn soon I was going to finally enjoy one of those special brownies. First, I had to get my bitches back. Chester was right. They were my heart.

I had no idea where Fletch and Slick were—yes, Fletch and Slick, because that's who they'd always be to me, even if I pronounced their proper names to their faces in the future because I was such a courteous bitch.

I didn't have much time left before Fletch would have to leave for the airport. The sun would start coming up around five thirty, but finally—finally!—the Happies party animals were slowing down from their park exploration. Most of them had set up camp in and around Pinata Village, settling onto blankets and portable lawn chairs, drinking wine coolers and watching the stars twinkle in the sky. The air had even calmed down. It was still warm, but not scorching, with a touch of rare, charmed humidity.

As I roamed the grounds, I felt supercharged. So much disaster had happened, so many of my worst fears realized. Yet I wouldn't deny it. I threw a great fucking party!

And Zeke had a thing for me? I kissed Zeke! I totally had a thing for Zeke!

I was giddy and ready to right the wrongs.

Zeke had gone off with Jason Dunker to check on Thrope, but his phone had no charge left anyway, and I needed to find my girls right away. They could be wandering anywhere in the theme park. They could even have left by now, but I felt confident they wouldn't while we were all sore. We were like an old threesome married unit that way. Never went to bed mad at each other. And one of us couldn't possibly jet all the way to Africa while still mad at the other two. In-flight diarrhea would be preferable to that outcome.

I approached Mega-Joan for help, pointing to her megaphone. "May I?"

"Have at it," said Mega-Joan, chomping down on a spicy pork taco. "I tell ya, we need to hire this food truck for our Las Vegas conventions. Incredible! I mean, if we can't eat in the Happies restaurant, eating from a food truck in the Happies theme park is surprisingly just as good! Don't tell Bev Happie I said, but better."

I placed the megaphone at my mouth, feeling Mega-Joan's power seep down into my vocal cords. No wonder she was so forceful. I needed to ask for one of these for Christmas. I announced into it, "Would Mercedes Zavala-Kim and Genesis Fletcher please report to the Mexican Seoul food truck in Pinata Village immediately? And if you are not Mercedes Zavala-Kim or Genesis Fletcher but you know where they are, please relay this message to them."

I put the megaphone down, thought better of relinquishing so much vocal power too soon, and then picked it back up for one additional message. "And tell Genesis Fletcher that taco'clock really is a fucking thing!"

Taco'clock really was a thing, and it was magic. It brought my true loves back to me. We sat on lawn chairs provided by the Happies, as the Happies prepared a final parade down Main Street to close out the night. Some of them were collecting sand and loose piñata ribbons as final keepsakes of the theme park land, while others sorted through candy bags, deciding which ones to throw to whoever stayed long enough for their parade.

"I'm sorry I bailed on you guys before we could talk it out more," I said. "I'm sorry for every single thing I did that made you mad and please let's not end this night still mad at each other. You guys are everything to me."

We attached hands in our semicircle, and squeezed. Hard. This would be the last one for a very long time.

"I'm sorry I freaked on both of you about leaving for Africa. . . ." Fletch loosened her hand from mine to look at the time on her phone. "Shit, in just a few hours. I gotta get home."

"I'm sorry I didn't tell you about my Vegas plans earlier," said Mercedes.

"Aren't you forgetting something?" Genesis said.

Mercedes said, "I'm not sorry about the Jake thing. That was fully reprehensible of both of you."

"You slept with *my* brother!" I reminded her.

"But he's not a jerk," said Mercedes. She gave us a look of disgust. "I thought you two would have better taste than to go for the obvious, shallow choice. I love Jake, but I would *never* want to see him dating one of my friends. Because he's kind of an asshole."

I gulped. "Um . . . announcement. I sort of have a thing for your *other* brother now?"

To my surprise, Mercedes clapped her hands in delight. "Zeke's had a crush on you since forever. I never said anything because he swore me to secrecy."

"Zeke? Really?" Fletch scrunched her face in disbelief, and then, as her brain processed the math, her mouth relaxed into a smile and she nodded. "That could work. Yeah. Yeah!"

"You let me think he was gay!" I said to Mercedes.

"No, *you* let yourself think that," she said. "He said he wanted you to figure it out yourself and he made me promise not to tell." She paused, and gave me the evil eye. "By the way, if you hurt him, I will hunt you down and kill you."

I started to cry. I couldn't help it. "I know!" I sobbed.

"It's okay!" said Fletch, tackling me into a hug. "Lots of girls don't realize a guy is straight."

"That's not why I'm crying! I just love you both so much and I can't believe you're both going to leave me here all alone."

"But you're going to San Francisco," said Fletch.

"Maybe she's not anymore?" said Mercedes.

Maybe she was right. I was definitely reconsidering. That girl always knew me best.

"Wow," said Fletch. She reached into my open bag and pulled out that damned napkin-wrapped food I'd been looking for all night! "Here, have a brownie. You've earned it."

That other girl also knew me best.

I unwrapped the napkin, but before I took a bite into

delicious, I thought of all the surprising treats Rancho had to offer. Taco'clock. My weird and sweet brother. Tunics of Virility. My classmates who weren't skipping town and who'd be fun to hang out with more. Happies—not just the place, which would be gone, but the sash-loving, obsessive, admittedly dear people.

Zeke!

There was a lot to stay for in my nowhere desert town.

It was finally a proper party and not a random collection of craziness.

The majority of Happies and classmates still left in the park—or who hadn't passed out somewhere in the park—had congregated on the grounds near the Mexican Seoul truck at the entrance to Pinata Village. The truck was officially out of food, so Selena and Jon joined the girls and me as we sat on low-to-the-ground folding beach chairs that the Happies caravans had brought in.

There weren't extra chairs, so Slick and I gave the parents ours, and we sat on the ground at their feet. Someone had made light fixtures out of tin cans with hammer holes in them, and then placed lit votive candles inside the cans, giving the effect of more starry lights in our dark campgrounds. Those Happies knew how to hack the hell out of basic gear bought in a whirlwind Home Depot expedition. The effect was enchanting. Nobody should kill all

Happies. Somebody ought to give them their own damn cable TV show.

"Foot massage, Mommy?" Slick asked Selena.

"Yes, please. God, yes. So tired," said Selena.

Fletch said to me, "I'm not offering you and your barf feet a massage. Just to be clear."

"I love you, too," I told her.

As Slick massaged her mom's feet, Selena burst into tears. "Did I hurt you?" Slick asked.

"No," Selena sobbed. "It's just . . . two of my babies are leaving the nest."

"You kicked one of them out tonight," Slick pointed out. "You could take that back."

Jon said, "Sorry to say, but it needed to happen. Long overdue."

"Vic might stay in Rancho a little longer," Fletch told the Z-K parents.

"Thank God," said Selena. "She owes me a shit-ton of beer money and I don't think she should be allowed to leave our block till she's paid off that debt."

"Plus, Town Council meetings would be so boring without her," said Jon.

Selena waved her hand at me like she was the Queen of England. She imitated my overconfident voice as she proclaimed, "So many admirers, I don't know what to do with all the love."

Something about that hand wave sparked Mega-Joan, who was sitting close enough not to need to invoke the power of the megaphone. She called out, "Now I know why you look so familiar. You're Selena Zavala! Third runner-up in the last Miss Happies pageant ever!"

"You were a Miss Happie contestant?" Slick shrieked to her mom. "How did you never tell us that before?" She looked accusingly at her dad. "And why have we never seen photographic evidence?"

"It was a dare," Selena said. "From that guy." She pointed at Jon. "The guy who knocked me up and caused me to have the slightly protruding belly that cost me the bikini competition. Then after I had kids, I worried it was a bad feminist message. Mom in an objectifying pageant because a hot guy challenged her to enter the contest. So I never mentioned it."

"There are pictures though, somewhere?" Fletch asked hopefully.

Mega-Joan said, "I'll have 'em posted online by tomorrow afternoon." She tossed an empty water bottle and a black Sharpie pen to Selena. "Sign this for me?"

"Sure," said Selena, laughing.

Fletch stood up and addressed the group with her regal valedictorian stance. "I have a question for all you guys who remember the old Happies. I know why *I* loved it. Why did you?"

Delroy Cowpoke seemed to appear out of nowhere, and he sat himself in the middle of our circle like he was Santa Claus addressing the elves.

"Happies was for everybody," he said.

"A ghetto Disney," said a biker man wearing a Hawaiian shirt that anyone would recognize from the cover of last year's Tunics of Virility Christmas catalog, modeled by Jon Z-K. "I came from the barrio. Rough neighborhood. Poor. Looked down on by outsiders. But we were always welcomed here like we were old family friends."

"It worked because it didn't," said Delroy. "Happies was too small, too weird, in an inefficient, hot-as-hell location. But that ice cream!"

"Those piñatas!" said Mega-Joan. "Too much of a good thing made it great!"

The piñata relics—literally thousands of colorful ribbons strewn on the ground everywhere—validated her memory. I wish I'd been there to see it when it was a whole village of piñatas hanging from every tree branch. I wish I'd been there to enjoy so much candy inside the piñatas.

Could the Dunk's brownie I'd just ingested be *that* quickly hallucinogenic? Because immediately after swallowing the last bite, I thought I saw a lightning bolt flash in the sky. "Holy shit!" I exclaimed. "Did I just see what I thought I saw?"

Another white light cracked in the sky. I knew by the surprised gasps in the crowd that it was real and not just the brownie.

But this was nearly summer. In the desert. During a drought. Impossible.

"The ghosts of Rancho Soldado have come calling," said Selena. "They wouldn't let the last night at Happies go by without letting us know they were up there partying, too. And mad as hell about what's going to happen to this sacred land."

I had utter respect for the ghosts of Rancho Soldado, but I really would have appreciated them holding off on the lightning until after the park grounds were cleared out. I'd been putting out minor fires all night and was finally able to enjoy myself. A lightning strike now would be highly inconvenient, about the worst fire hazard this park could have in its final hours, except for fireworks.

And then there were fireworks.

Pop! Pop! Pop! The sparklers exploded high into the sky from Main Street in bursts of gold, silver, blues, and reds.

"Looks like your new boyfriend is ready to fire up the band!" Slick told me.

"Huh?" I said. I'd had boys but never an actual boyfriend. The thought that Zeke could be my first was crazy. Possibly amazing.

"Zeke never starts a show without fireworks," said Jon.

"God help us," said Selena, doing the sign of the cross over her chest.

Zeke and I had only just kissed, and already I wanted to throttle my new maybe boyfriend.

CHAPTER

26

LOS YUNKEROS TAUNT THE SKY GODS

4:30 a.m.

The Chug Bug destruction had been a teaser. This town had an ancient curse hanging over it, and I knew those ghosts wouldn't let the night end without them giving my party a last epic blaze.

I just hadn't expected the fires would come from Zeke.

When the fireworks erupted, it was impossible for the party not to shift to where they'd come from.

The crowds gathered by the Mexican Seoul truck made the quick walk over to Main Street. I cursed Zeke under my breath as I charged toward the new party center with everyone else.

"Don't worry so hard, General Nav," said Slick as we reached Main. "The guys are experienced firecracker launchers. Except for that one time at the Our Lady of Guadalupe Hispanic Heritage block party."

"What happened?"

"You don't want to know," said Slick, making the sign of the cross over her chest.

Their fireworks preshow complete, the musical sounds of Los Yunkeros commenced. A punk-Mexified version of a very appropriate song opened the show. Trumpet, violin, and Zeke's voice, singing, *"Well we got no choice / All the girls and boys."*

It seemed like everyone in the park (that wasn't rightfully locked up, sorry Miss Ann Thrope) had found their way to this spot, and they picked up the next battle cry along with Zeke. *"Makin' all that noise / 'Cause they found new toys."*

The girls and I sang along as we reached the "stage" where Los Yunkeros played, on wood shipping pallets stacked three-high that they must have found in the back of the restaurant. Los Yunkeros wore mariachi outfits, but theirs leaned more to late '70s disco, with purple bell-bottom polyester pants lined with gold brocade on the sides, frilly purple pirate shirts rimmed in gold collars and gold buttons, and purple and gold handkerchiefs around their necks. There was Zeke on vihuela guitar, his buddy

Tommy on trumpet, and their other buddy Humberto on violin.

And then there were even more intense lightning bolts, now with added thunder rumbles, to accompany the band. Everyone sang out, *"School's out for summer / School's out forever!"*

I was a little bit baked and so hot, tired, and fired up, that I screamed along with everyone else like Los Yunkeros were the Beatles at Shea Stadium during the Paleolithic rock 'n' roll era. The sky demanded the screams. Lightning strikes were acts of God, and God knows there was nothing I could do to stop them anymore.

As Los Yunkeros performed, a group of my classmates hauled a new creation into the middle of the mosh pit that had formed in front of the makeshift stage. From a distance, it looked like it could be a pharaoh's head on an Egyptian pyramid. Up close, it was a more locally sourced piece of art: an effigy of Miss Ann Thrope, made with materials that could not have been more flammable. The effigy was led forth by the arty and rad contingents of Rancho Soldado's High School graduating class, who carried her over with the mischievous irony of a Cersei-level walk of shame. The artists must have disassembled the Tiki Hut in the Lovers Lane mini-golf course to make her, because her armless torso was crafted with bamboo sticks that could only have come from there. The sticks were fastened together with pieces of desert creosote bush. Her face was their masterwork. Her ears were the driver's and passenger's side mirrors from the Chug Bug, and her eyes were a collection of beer bottle caps formed in circular shapes above her nose, made from the VW bus's relic gear stick shift. From the smell, I judged her hair to have been made with sagebrush scrub that had been spray-painted yellow; it was the same paint color that was used to graffiti a slogan across her bamboo-and-creosote chest: *Not Maybe. Will.*

"Should we burn her?" Leticia Johnson called out.

"Not maybe! Will!" my classmates in the crowd shouted.

The Happies, who could not have known Thrope's catchphrase for detention and failing grade warnings, joined in anyway for the next wave of chanting.

"Burning Wo-man! Burning Wo-man!"

Zeke lifted the mike to his mouth—a mouth I wanted to reconnect with at the first available opportunity—and his eyes found me in the audience. I don't know how they did it, but Los Yunkeros managed to keep performing, vibing off the crowd's energy, getting sweatier, louder, more intense with each note. They didn't pause between songs, but jumped right into the next one, as the crowd cheered the opening notes of a familiar and favorite song, and then Zeke crooned directly at me: *"I never meant to cause you any sorrow / I never meant to cause you any pain."*

The crowd roared its approval. Not only did Los Yunkeros not suck, they were on fire! I wanted to add to it.

I only wanted one time to see you laughing.

That meant me, too!

Suddenly, with no forewarning, I was lifted onto the shoulders of Olivier Farkas. I yelped in surprise, and fear, and had to grab onto Olivier's hair to keep my balance. "What are you doing, Olivier?" I demanded.

He didn't answer, but walked me right next to the probably ten-foot-high effigy. Troy Ferguson threw a grill lighter up into the air for me to catch. "The class has elected you to do the honors!" Troy shouted over the music and the crowd's cheers.

Zeke sang, *"I only want to see you / Underneath the purple rain,"* and it was like he was telling me the fire would be okay. I thought of how many more fires our future kisses would stoke.

I thought of staying in Rancho when Bev and Happies restaurant were no longer here and that unrepentant fuckwad Thrope was mayor. I thought of all the petty detentions, misdemeanors, and bad grades Thrope had foisted on her students—in particular the Navarro kids. I thought of all the Town Council meetings she'd obstructed—particularly the one where I'd laid out my soul into a damn good plan for revitalizing my town instead of driving it to become a wastoid epicenter of scheming corporate profit. I thought of how no matter how hard you try to do the right thing, to be good and fair and decent, it often didn't matter against so much of the suck in the world. I thought of how dry that brownie had been, but damn had it moistened my ambition for anarchy.

"Catch!" Jason Dunker called to me. "Leftovers! Comped, for you." With my free hand, I caught a small brown baby 'shroom.

Fuck fire safety.

It was like a movie in slo-mo where my mind warned *nooooooo* . . .

But my heart said *yesssssssss*.

I bit.

I lit.

CHAPTER **27** THE MORNING AFTER

8 a.m.

I was crooned awake. *I can't leave you alone / You got me feenin'!* My eyes reluctantly blinked open, and I looked around, but saw no Zeke singing to me. My heart fell. His was the face I wanted to see first thing in the morning. But I did see my phone on the ground, next to me, lit up with a call from Zeke, who'd apparently also set a new ringtone for me. I couldn't reach the phone, being that one of my hands was handcuffed to Miss Ann Thrope, and the other to a jail cell bar. And my head was kinda killing me.

What. The. Fuck?

The call ended, and then a text appeared from Zeke: I'll swing by to pick you up in an hour. Mercedes sent me to drop off Fletch at her house so she can make her flight. Shake it off, Z

Thrope groaned next to me. Rewind. I was handcuffed to Thrope! High holy hell!

Slowly it was coming back to me. Before the concert had broken out, Jason Dunker had been sent to give the prisoner a slice of magic mushroom pizza. One of the last moments I remembered was him saying Thrope had only eaten a few bites of her prison food—enough to down just *part* of her magic snack. The Dunk didn't want to see the magic go to waste, so he salvaged the mushroom bit leftover, and saved it for later, when he tossed it up to me as I was about to light the Thrope effigy on fire. The Dunk thought Thrope and me sharing from the same 'shroom was "poetic justice."

Now, as my eyes came more into focus in the daylight, I saw Slick and Chester sitting on the ground on Main Street, a few feet away from the UnHappies Jail. They saw me stir. "Good morning, precious," Slick called to me.

"What the . . ." I started to say.

Slick came over and held her phone up on the other side of the jail bars for me to see. "It's too much to explain," she said. "Here, just watch the supercut."

"It's already gotten five hundred eighteen views on YouTube," said Chester.

Over the song "Purple Rain," there was me, dancing around the Burning Wo-Man. Topless. Not braless, thankfully.

I reached my free hand to touch my chest and looked down. My red bra was still on. My shirt was not.

"You're gonna miss the best part!" said Slick.

I returned my gaze to her phone. There was the sudden swell of rain that Zeke's song, and the ghosts of Rancho Soldado, miraculously provided. There was me, rolling around in the moist, charred embers of the effigy.

"Was the fire department here?" I asked. I touched my face. There was no mirror, but I could feel how dirty, and probably charred, my face was. The sting in my eyes told me they were bloodshot. I must have looked as bad as I felt.

"Oh yeah," said Chester. "But the rain had pretty much put out the fire by then."

"The fire department didn't shut down the party?"

"They were going to, but the rain had already done their work. And they wanted to see the final parade when the Happies marched down Main Street at dawn."

"No!" I cried out. "I can't believe I missed it! Was it amazing?"

Slick said, "I'll show you that cut when you're not so

hungover. I don't want to make you more sick over what you missed."

The most important question: "How the fuck did I end up in UnHappies Jail?"

Chester said, "You were exhausted. Overstimulated. Tripping."

Slick said, "Cra-cra-*crazy*. Now don't kill yourself, but when you started rolling around in the embers, Evergrace Everdell was actually the one who saved your ass."

"Everbitch saved *me*? Doubtful."

Chester said, "Shocking, but true."

Slick said, "Evergrace performed what she called a 'Random Act of Compassion.' She made a citizen's arrest of you, and put you in here, handcuffed to Thrope."

"You *let* that happen?" I asked them.

Slick said, "Everyone agreed it was for the best."

Chester added, "Including the CHP."

Fuck! "CHP was *also* here?"

Slick said, "Hell yeah. They were pretty nice about the whole thing, in the end. They told the drunk and tripping kids to roll themselves down the Ravishing Ravine, because the bottom of it was technically Nevada land where they had no jurisdiction to prosecute. And by then no one was really fist-fighting or vandalizing anything anymore."

"Don't tell me," I said. "The CHP wanted to see the last parade, too."

"Yup," said Chester.

Slick gave Chester a look, and then nodded at him. He reluctantly pulled a piece of paper from his back pocket and flashed it at me through the jail bars.

"What's that?"

Chester said, "A summons. For you to appear in court to answer charges of trespassing, instigating disorderly conduct, violating fire laws. Shit like that."

"OH, FUCK."

Slick said, "They could have arrested you. 'OH, I'M LUCKY' is more like it."

Thrope started to stir, her body moving, her mouth babbling "Wha? What? Wh . . . where?"

"I gotta go," said Slick. "Mom said she'll make a hangover batch of chilaquiles for you when you get home."

Chester said, "I'll leave a fresh bottle of Advil by your bed. You're welcome."

Theirs was the ultimate betrayal. I shrieked, "You guys can't leave me here like this! With Thrope!"

"You two have shit to work out," said Slick.

Chester said, "Good luck!"

In tandem, they made the sign of the cross over their respective chests.

Thrope's bite of magic must not have totally worn off yet because she half-smiled in my direction. "Mornin'," she said.

She was in such a relaxed mood. My head hurt so bad, and I didn't want to form more words, but I'd probably never have the opportunity to get a real answer from her again. I said, "Why *do* you hate Happies so much? Why be in a Miss Happies pageant—and win!—if you loathe the place?"

Thrope sighed, and she put her index finger to her mouth, spitting drool as she spoke. "Shhh! I didn't win fair and square. I was first runner-up. My mistake for trying to have the winner's hula grass skirt and hula top disqualified as a legitimate bathing suit competition entry."

"What difference did that make?"

"Because when they held the do-over, the bikini contest revealed *she* was a *he*. I had been named runner-up to a man. I *hate* being second, but especially to a man. I served my term as Miss Happie like a good soldier, but I've hated the place ever since."

"So why didn't you leave Rancho Soldado?" I asked Thrope.

"Why didn't *you*?" she said. "You brats should have left town with your man-stealing mother."

I was strangely comforted by her attack. All these years I'd thought maybe it was my imagination that she was so mean to us over something my siblings and I had no control over. The bad grades and the thwarting me at Town Council meetings hadn't been because I was dumb or misinformed, as I'd sometimes secretly feared. It really was personal. That's how Thrope played her politics. To the bone.

Politics needed to change in this town.

Outside our jail cell, there was a zombie walk of hungover kids and Happies trudging down Main Street toward the exit at Clown Town. Too tired to stop to engage the prisoners on display in conversation, they simply acknowledged us with thumbs-up signs and cries of "Great party, Vic!" and "See ya at inauguration, Mayor Thrope!"

Mega-Joan had rallied a chain gang, I mean volunteer crew, to clean up bottles and other litter along Main Street. At the giant fallen clown, I could see Mayor Jerry handing out cigars and coupons for his Tunics of Virility store to people as they exited the park.

"It's a girl!"

"Congrats, dude!"

I expected Delroy Cowpoke to come by and unlock devil Thrope and me from the handcuffs at any moment, but instead the warden turned out to be Bev Happie. She stood over us outside the UnHappies Jail cell. She said, "I guess you two made quite a fucking ruckus last night."

Clearly regaining her senses, Thrope spat, "Victoria made a mess of it. Not me. How could you authorize this debacle, Bev? You could have put the whole real estate deal in jeopardy."

Bev said, "Maybe I wanted to."

Wait. What? Bev was reconsidering the deal?

Bev released us from the handcuffs. Thrope and I both shook our hands and arms wildly to get the circulation going again. Bev threw me a dirty old Happies dishwashers' T-shirt to cover up my chest, bare except for the bra holding in Ezra and Esme. I put on the shirt. It stunk so good. Like Happies.

"Where *were* you last night?" Thrope snarled at Bev.

Bev said, "I was so stressed about signing Happies away, the doc gave me a gawddamn happy pill to settle down, not like that's your fucking business. Knocked me the hell out for the night. But I woke up with a new lease on life. And now I see all these wonderfully crazy Happies here, and all this mess here, all these remnants of laughter and good energy, and I remember my grandparents' joy in this place and in their customers. They're Happies. I'm a Happie. We're a family. And maybe I don't feel like selling after all."

"You have to!" said Thrope. "What would you retire on? Can't live on goodwill, lady."

"I don't need much to live on," said Bev. "And I only just graduated high school. My life's just starting. If some overseas businessmen want to buy this land for way less than it's fucking worth, why can't I find investors on my own to reinvigorate Happies for the next generation?"

I said, "Exactly! We could modernize the park but still keep its old charm! Install Mexican Seoul taco trucks throughout, and have a mosh pit dance hall, and piñata art festivals, and holed-up tin can light fixtures, and—"

"This business is useless," interrupted Thrope. "Last night was about nostalgia and anarchy. Those two things can't finance Happies into the future. The land is all that's of value here. For God's sake, we've talked about this a million times, Bev. *No one wants to buy the business.*"

Mayor Jerry stopped by and handed Bev a cigar. He said, "I might like to. Now that I'm a dad, I'd like to leave my kid something great. Much as I love my shirt store, it doesn't have the same history—or devoted following—as Happies. I got a few mil to spare, give or take some poorly performing mutual funds."

Bev's eyes widened in awe. "My horoscope in the

Death Valley Psychic News said I could expect help from mutual friends!"

"Nonsense!" Thrope spewed.

A mayor doing right by his town? Bev might stick around? Maybe Rancho Soldado wasn't a wastoid place with no future. Maybe it had some hope after all!

"It's the best thing that could happen to reinvigorate Rancho's economy—using our unique resources and local talent to put us back on the map," I told Thrope.

"Will you shut up already, Victoria?" Thrope said. "That's what I've been trying to do all along. Strengthen this town's economy! Demolish this useless institution and use the land to rebuild Rancho Soldado from the ground up—bigger and better."

"No, I won't shut up," I said to Thrope. "Why can't you be more encouraging, just for once? Why don't you put aside your selfish interests for the needs of this town?"

Thrope rolled her eyes. "Not that again, Victoria. Give it up already. You and I both know there's no one who cares more about this town than me."

"Except *me*. I have so many ideas for what a new Happies theme park could be like. I'll help you find additional investors, Bev!"

Thrope said, "If you know so well what's best for this town, maybe *you* ought to run for mayor, you naive teenage idiot."

Lindsay was gonna kill me when I didn't make it to San Francisco next week. I never listen to that dumbslut.

I smiled at Thrope. Genuinely. Gratefully. She'd just given me my life.

I said, "Not maybe. *Will.*"